Fear and Money
Isabelle Graw

Fear and Money
A Novel
Isabelle Graw

Sternberg Press

Everything that is described in these pages occurred in one way or another. But no person, no place, and no event should be taken for the reality.
—Ulrike Edschmid, *The Disappearance of Philip S.*

Je crois que tout le monde est angoissé.
—Bernard Buffet

Last night I lay awake for a long time again. I've felt so worn down recently that, in desperation, I gave in and ordered a weighted blanket. For weeks now, my Facebook feed has been touting it as the solution to my sleep problems—probably as a result of me googling "insomnia" too many times. And so, last night, I finally admitted defeat and clicked the "buy" button, in the hope that this blanket will grant me more peaceful nights and spare me the torturous hours spent tossing and turning on my mattress. It just arrived. I carefully take it out of the packaging—it smells strangely synthetic, and the cover feels scratchy and uncomfortable. I decide to put a fresh duvet cover on it, and to lay it over my legs and torso, up to my neck. I chose a light blanket, just six kilos, to match my weight, but the pressure on my body feels far heavier. The blanket positively buries me, preventing any movement; I feel totally immobilized, as if I were strapped down to an operating table. How this blanket, of all things, is supposed to soothe anxiety and promote sleep is a mystery to me. Its weight forces the body into rigor mortis, which I instinctively react to by kicking it away from me. As a result, I'm now wide awake and in a state of high alert—despite this being the time when I should actually be sleeping. I decide to calm down by meditating for a while. A few weeks ago, I began trying out various guided meditations aimed at improving sleep. I got hung up on watching the videos of a "guide" named Peter, whose deep, sonorous voice promised calming effects. Since Peter has the habit of bizarrely drawing out each individual word, however, his meditations take some getting used to, and I often find myself unable to stifle a laugh while listening to him. Peter offers a range of different meditation videos, depending on whether you're looking to find peace, reduce stress, or banish your fears. In dealing with rising feelings of anxiety, for example, he advises against trying to fight or "get rid" of these feelings, arguing that it's better to consciously perceive them and, with this, create an inner distance from them. While I attempt to adopt this observational perspective on my own anxieties, I also ask myself how I'm supposed to take an "outside" view of a feeling that fills me up so entirely. It rises in my chest, dominating my entire self-image. Freud was right when he declared the ego to be "the actual seat of anxiety"—as a site, that is, where this anxiety not only resides but is also generated. And it's this "ego"—the operating system of anxiety, according to Freud—that I'm now supposed to escape through meditation? Peter seems to see fear as something that can be separated from the ego and brought under control through observation, yet my fear is so deeply rooted in my body and my spirit that I'm unable to distance myself from it in this way. I mentally reject Peter's meditation instructions, my body now feeling more irritated than ever under the horribly heavy therapy blanket. I'm unable to guide my attention to my breathing, as Peter suggests; instead, I lie frozen under this monstrosity of a blanket, which, far from easing my fears and relaxing me as promised, makes me absolutely frantic. I have to rid myself of this blanket and return it.

    I experienced something similar during an MRI scan yesterday, which I was forced to endure after suffering from months of intense pain in my lower back. I was locked inside a tube that narrowly surrounded my body during the scan, stretched out flat as if practicing corpse pose. I felt a particular sense of foreboding the moment I slowly glided into the tube on my "stretcher," like a dead body being shoved into a refrigerator at a morgue. The only things connecting me to life outside this tubular tomb were the ear-splitting techno noises made by the machine, which I tried to focus on as I lay there with my eyes closed. But even the loud pounding was unable to distract me from the fact that I was actually in wild panic, with my heart racing and a cramp in my chest. I desperately clung on to the alarm button they had given me in case I felt unable to bear it anymore, well aware that pressing it would only draw out the torturous process longer than necessary. Time passed at a snail's pace, stretching out toward infinity in my panic. I was rigid with fear; my whole being seemed to be made of fear, as Kafka put it in one of his letters to Milena. This was made worse by the fact that during an MRI scan—unlike during angst-filled sleepless nights—it isn't possible to simply stand up and leave the "bed." You're stuck there in the tube. I now find myself in a similar situation thanks to the wretched therapy blanket: It pushes me down into the bed and deprives me of my mobility, attempting to force me into peace and relaxation while actually producing the opposite effect—namely, resistance. Resolving to free myself of this monster blanket, I heave it off and walk into the kitchen to make myself a cup of sleep-promoting herbal tea.

Thanks to the tea, I did fall asleep at some point, only to be jolted awake again—it's now 3 a.m., the middle of the night.

I quickly calculate the time in New York, where my boyfriend, Antoine, lives. There, it's 9 p.m.—the start of his social program for the evening, which I'm unable to participate in from here in Berlin. For me to call him now might be interpreted as an attempt to control him. But I also know from experience that only his reassuring words can ease the fear of loss I already feel rising within me. I need his reassurance, since without it, I'm damned to spend the entire night imagining the pleasures and infidelities he might be enjoying without me. Sleep is out of the question in this state. Instead, I mentally revisit parties we attended together in New York, where I couldn't escape the impression that some of the heterosexual women present were merely waiting for me to fly back to Berlin and disappear from his life again. They would practically fall over him, signaling their readiness to step in at any time, should he ever want to replace me with a more "convenient" girlfriend—one who lives near him, that is, and who doesn't require him to be in a long-distance relationship. Reflecting on these experiences, I convince myself that there might actually be objective reasons for my fear of him leaving me, and that I'm therefore entitled to the reassurance of a phone call. Having thus granted myself the license to call him, I reach for my phone and dial his number. As so often, I only reach his voicemail. The rest of the night promises to be torture. In a few minutes I'll try again, then repeatedly call him in ever-decreasing intervals. I'll ask myself why he's not hearing his phone, and if he might be deliberately ignoring me. And the more worked up I get at the idea of him enjoying himself without me, the more urgent my need for his words of reassurance will become. I'll slide into a panic attack without an "I love you" from him. Why won't he take pity on me and call me back? After at least twenty attempts, I decide to retaliate by making myself unavailable. I deposit my phone at the other end of my apartment, so I won't hear it ringing or vibrating, then I return to bed. Lying there, I do my best to feel that I'm self-sufficient, and to find the inner peace that some of my friends astonishingly manage to possess. They're enough for themselves and don't get thrown into a panic by unanswered phone calls. How did I slip into this destructive dependency on an absent man? It would be laughable if I couldn't fall asleep without his reassuring words. My obsessive fixation on him is beneath me, and I have to overcome it as soon as possible. And yet the longer I lie in bed trying to cope with this anxiety on my own, the more other worries force their way into my consciousness—in addition to my fear of losing my boyfriend, I'm now also occupied by my financial problems.

First to arrive in my thoughts is my terrible landlord, who's currently plaguing me with excessive demands. He claims that the heating costs for my apartment have tripled due to a new provider, and that he therefore has to charge me €400 more each month up front for utility costs in the future. Such a large increase would strain me financially. I just don't know where I'm supposed to find this money. It's notoriously hard to earn anything significant writing books, unless you produce a bestseller—

somewhat unlikely in my case, given my chosen subject matter and writing style. Other potential sources of income, such as jobs in the auction sphere, are hard to find and would require me to reposition myself professionally. Any such activities would also put my symbolic capital as an independent critic in jeopardy. Saving's not an option either; I don't want to be constantly keeping track of what I spend. Unfortunately, my love of extravagant gestures means I often disregard my actual income level and eventually end up in financial trouble. I've been living beyond my means for a long time now. In addition, high levels of inflation mean my bank balance is currently losing value every day, and so I still get poorer even when I spend nothing at all. Sleepless, sweaty, and agitated, I go through strategies that might free me from my financial precarity. Perhaps I should enter the art market and earn money that way? Then again, it's not as if the collectors of the world are simply waiting for me to bless them with an interesting offer. Beyond this, the artistic positions that interest me carry little weight in the current art economy—the market gets on very well without them. Out of all the careers, why did I choose one that brings me such financial anxiety? In my younger years, I optimistically assumed that money would find its way to me one day; arrogant as I was, I felt I somehow deserved it. Having grown older, however, I now realize that the opposite might just as well be the case, that, as an older woman, I have lost any power I once had to attract money, which simply no longer finds its way to me. I feel this crunch in all areas of my professional life; even museums now refuse to pay the fees I demand for giving lectures. The deeper I sink into my money worries, the more problems emerge, and so I go from one crisis to the next. I decide to distract myself and calm down by reading for a while. My notorious insomnia means I've worked my way through an unfathomable syllabus of readings in recent years, and biographies have proven particularly effective in soothing my existential fears about my future. Entering into the lives of others relativizes my own problems. I reach for a biography of George Sand.

Apparently, I did fall asleep at some point. It's now 9 a.m., and far from being refreshed, I feel exhausted by the restless night. I forbid myself from going into the hallway to get my phone, delaying the moment when I see whether Antoine has tried to reach me or not, but I soon give in and grab it in resignation. There's only a single, icy text message, in which he wishes me "Good night." It's almost as if he were fulfilling a burdensome duty by writing these words—as if he were merely trying to get rid of me so he could carry on enjoying himself unencumbered. I tell myself that this kind of speculation will get me nowhere. I have to stop getting caught up in thinking about his life as a way of avoiding the reality of my everyday existence in Berlin—there's so much to be done, after all! But I have no energy or drive, partly because of my lack of sleep. I'm simply too shattered to valiantly jump under the shower and start the day, and so I lie down on the bed with my phone and begin scrolling through Instagram and Facebook. I've repeatedly resolved to break this bad habit, but I reflexively take my phone into bed with me each morning, nonetheless.

While this is tantamount to the behavior of an addict, I rationalize it with the idea that it connects me to others—the great promise of social media. Except that, unlike physical meetings with my friends, I draw no strength from reading their status updates; on the contrary, this bleak online culture of self-marketing (which I myself admittedly engage in on occasion) just depresses me and makes it even harder to find the motivation to face the day. Once I've finally managed to tear myself away from my phone, I shower and sit down at my desk, where I force myself to banish any thoughts of my faithless boyfriend, and where I'm magically able to transform myself into an efficient workhorse capable of blocking out its heartache. I work through my to-do list at rapid speed, writing emails, correcting passages of text, and organizing meetings in a hyperactive rush. On closer inspection, this intensive way of working can also be traced back to anxiety: the anxiety of what might happen if I stop. I recently read Fritz Riemann's *Grundformen der Angst* (*Anxiety: Using Depth Psychology to Find a Balance in Your Life*) and found myself identifying with his description of the "compulsive character," who obsessively plans out their life in an attempt to bring it under control. I begin each year with a list of "work goals," for example, and I take great satisfaction in gradually ticking off my achievements. According to Riemann, it's the deep-rooted fear of death within each of us that compulsive characters like myself are attempting to ward off with our zealous planning, perpetual activism, and craving for control. In his view, however, the compulsive character pays a high price for being constantly busy and leaving nothing to chance, since life with all its contingencies passes them by as a result. Anyone who compulsively plans out their days misses out on numerous opportunities in life, Riemann claims. By cramming as much as I can into my daily schedule, sitting at my desk each morning before dutifully fulfilling my exercise quota in the evening, I close myself off to whatever might come my way from outside: I no longer even perceive the unexpected, and so life passes me by. According to Riemann, this mania for activity and control conceals a deep-seated "fear of death," which the psychoanalyst Melanie Klein declared to be the origin of fear in general. For Klein, a life without fear is unimaginable, in part because our unconscious is itself defined by our "fear of annihilation." Since the unconscious cannot be governed, however, this fear of our own destruction is as uncontrollable as it is threatening. I know exactly what Klein means by this—I, too, experience my fears as entirely overwhelming, since they all stem from this primal fear of annihilation and destruction.

I instinctively think of Peter, my meditation guide, who makes the opposite claim in his videos. He tries to convince his listeners that they don't need to be afraid—that they're not actually in danger but *safe*. I'm immune to such rationalizing attempts at pacification, however, which might be due to the fact that the border between "objective" and "neurotic" fear is fluid, as Klein also writes. According to her, it's impossible to draw a clear distinction between neurotic fears and dangerous situations that legitimately trigger fear, meaning there's always an objective aspect to my ostensibly neurotic fears, while those that are objectively justified are informed, in turn, by elements of my neurosis. I only need to read about the rapidly rising gas prices or the impact of inflation on the value of money, for example, and my inner fears are unleashed anew. But the fact that I'm so sensitive to *these* external triggers in particular is partly due to my neurotic, anxious disposition. Specific fear-triggering events in the outside world resonate with my own character and experiences. In the depths of my being, for instance, I harbor the fear that I might suffer the same fate as my father, who lost everything he had in his early sixties; the fear of ending up in poverty in old age is thus my constant companion. I read an interview with the writer Martin Walser somewhere in which he argues that money is the cure for anxiety, and that anyone who has it is immunized against fear. This is untrue, of course—in my experience wealthy people are often extremely scared by the idea that their money might be taken away from them, or that they could end up with financial difficulties. But this is hardly the case with me: Like Walser, having money considerably reduces my anxiety. If a well-paid commission means a larger sum does reach my account for once, instead of just the usual endless debits leaving it, then I clearly sense how this calms me inside. Should I earn less, however, then every thought of my disappearing bank balance triggers feelings of panic. I consciously avoid reading my balance if I'm forced to make a bank transfer in such a situation, since the strain of acknowledging it would be too much and set off an anxiety attack. My heart pounding, I ignore my current "takings" and hurry through the transfer, getting it out of the way as quickly as possible. Every time before I log in, I also worry that my money might have been debited by someone, or that it has simply vanished into the digital ether. In part, it is because of these fears—as irrational as they admittedly are—that I put off doing my banking duties for as long as possible. I recently went five weeks without logging in to my account at all, not daring to look at my balance until my anxiety had been sufficiently brought under control.

Money is also a factor when it comes to choosing my relationships; I'll admit that one reason I'm so strongly attracted to Antoine is that his high income as a financial adviser promises a degree of security. Despite my left-wing convictions, I'm still essentially a material girl at heart—it's one of the central contradictions that make me who I am. For all of Antoine's endearing qualities— like his attentiveness, his sensitivity, and his winning smile—it's not these traits alone that draw me to him. I also admire his equally tasteful and expensive lifestyle, with its carefully selected high-end furniture, designer labels, and vintage Porsche that he regularly picks me up from JFK in when I visit him in New York. Since my father also drove a Porsche before his financial debacle, I feel totally secure in this car, as if nothing at all could happen to me while I'm sitting in it. But my experience with my father also makes me painfully aware how illusory this security is; there was certainly no security when he quickly married another woman after divorcing my mother. The Porsche thus triggers ambivalent feelings within me: a sense of security coupled with a fear of loss. The latter manifests itself in extreme agitation and nervousness in Antoine's company, and I constantly predict the end of our relationship, making calmness and serenity an unachievable state. Staying at his carefully styled apartment in New York always makes me feel as if I were back in the villa of my early childhood: Everything seems to be in order, and yet this order is also tangibly under threat. For as I know from experience, the happiness that is bestowed upon me here will not last. That my relationship with Antoine is a long-distance one only fuels my fears, which rise to extreme levels in his absence. The fact that we live on different continents means I often ultimately have no idea what he's doing, or where he is; he could have long ago lost interest in me and be off amusing himself somewhere, without me even having had a chance to realize it. Perhaps he really has already replaced me with someone else. The problem with envisioning such scenarios is that they are then highly likely to become self-fulfilling prophecies. It's often the case that the thing we fear the most does actually happen, and so it seems inevitable that my worst anxiety dreams will come true—that he'll get together with another woman over in New York. He's often complained that I'm not there with him, while his friends all have their lovers by their sides. On the other hand, hasn't he always also assured me that I'm his great love? Lying in bed one time after sex, he even admitted to me that he sometimes thanks God for our relationship, despite not believing in him otherwise. So, he sees me as a gift from God!

I glance at the clock. It's 6 a.m. over in New York, and I know from experience that Antoine will be slowly heading off to the gym around now to complete his daily workout—together with his personal trainer, of course. I consider giving him a quick call, to wish him "good morning" in loving and spuriously casual tones. In truth, of course, I want to know what happened last night, where he was, and who he met. Were any potential rivals there? Why do I find it so hard to trust him? I'd like to be able to give him the benefit of the doubt while still "remaining true to myself," as they always say in yoga. Every attempt I make at practicing this maxim fails, however, since remaining true to myself means being instantly invaded by a wealth of worries and fears from both outside and within. My "self" is a turbulent place, shot through with external experiences and thought spirals. My thoughts spring back to Antoine again, and so I spontaneously call him—and he actually answers this time!

    While my conversation with him is short, it still brings me some relief. He and a friend attended an opening yesterday evening before moving on to a party, during which he supposedly missed me and longed for me to be there with him. He also claims to be looking forward to me visiting him in a few weeks. We briefly discuss the negative environmental implications of long-distance relationships like our own; our frequent long-haul flights can no longer be justified in the face of the climate crisis, and Antoine remarks that we'll need to find another solution in the long run. I'm reassured by the fact that he sees us sharing a future together, even if my anxiety means there's a lingering skepticism. Now feeling less agitated, I'm able to turn to my work in lighter spirits. But before I can, I'm thrown off balance by a worrying thought: While I take every opportunity I can to travel to New York, he rarely visits me in Berlin, and then only for two or three days at most at a time. He claims he could only live and work in New York, and when he was offered a position in Berlin recently, he automatically turned it down. He apparently assumes I would do anything to maintain our bond, but this clearly doesn't mean the same applies to him. Our relationship is asymmetrical in this respect, and I undoubtedly do more for it than he does. It's not in my nature to see matters of love in such calculating terms, however. Isn't it normal for one person to put in more effort and make more concessions in a relationship? I also can't allow myself to forget how much emotional intensity and attention I get from Antoine when we do see each other. And beyond this, there's the fact that Berlin has little to offer those who, like him, work in finance. There's nothing to be gained for him here. And yet I still feel the resentment rising in me when I think of how often he has overturned our shared travel plans or shortened or delayed his visits to Berlin. He's clearly not ready to make space for our love in his life— he essentially wants things to remain the same, but with me added on top. That there's a gendered dimension to this storyline is also obvious: As so often, it's me, the "woman," who puts in more of the work and turns her whole life upside down, while he sees our relationship as a sort of surplus to what he had before. He lives his life over there in New York, waiting for me to come to him, without making any concessions to me. I'm neither willing nor able to give up everything for him, however. Apart from the fact that I would have to leave my treasured circle of friends in Berlin, taking such a step would also have serious financial consequences. I would become completely financially dependent on him, since I would lose my job here and have to rebuild my professional life from the bottom up, which wouldn't be easy in New York. The mere thought of this frightens me. Or am I just using this rationalization as an excuse, since in reality I'm afraid of commitment and fundamentally unwilling to give myself over to this relationship?

It's unsettling how much I obsess over Antoine, as if constantly thinking about him (and us) meant I could somehow hold onto him. I pull myself together and return to my duties. I know from experience that immersing myself in my work is an effective antidote against rising fears of loss. Structure also helps: The more tightly scheduled my day is, with clearly defined working hours for writing and regular exercise sessions, the less room my endless fantasies about Antoine's life in New York occupy in my head. Ultimately, I only know him as a projection of myself. But who is he really? No idea!

My diary serves an important function in this context: Bound in wine-red leather and written by hand, it contains dates and deadlines that pull me out of my fixation on Antoine. But as soon as the distraction of the meeting (or whatever else) is gone, I feel an immediate sense of inner unease that makes me quickly reach for my phone to check if he's been in touch. If there's no message, panic starts to set in: Could he have ghosted me? I force myself to continue working through my to-do list in these moments, which keeps him at bay for a while and allows me to concentrate on the tasks at hand. But the fact that I've found it increasingly difficult to stay focused recently is not exclusively down to my thoughts of my boyfriend over in New York. There are also all the disturbing online news stories that I'm unable to avoid, like the arrival of a new (and supposedly extremely infectious) variant of the coronavirus or the devastating consequences of the ongoing war of aggression in Ukraine. Bad tidings like these fuel my fears and bring me to a standstill, above all in my writing. I'm unable to shield myself from world events, which I feel a connection with. I'm particularly unsettled by the articles on *Spiegel Online*, which deliberately stoke certain fears in order to get more clicks. Fortunately, the most alarming articles are hidden behind a paywall, as with one titled "Inflation Shock: We've Never Felt So Afraid." This headline alone is enough to make me tremble. And yet as soon as I limit my news consumption and focus strictly on my work tasks, the reality of life beyond my desk loses its power to throw me off track—it's as if, by writing, I take shelter from the same world my work feeds off. Only by distancing myself from all that immediately triggers my anxiety am I able to make any progress with my work. Even on holiday, I stick to my morning routine instead of letting myself drift away—my colleagues can still reach me at any time, and my professional responsibilities continue as usual. At the same time, my body signals to me that I have to stop constantly forging career plans and wallowing in problems, communicated via sleepless nights that are particularly acute at the beginning of the vacation. While it's clear I'm demanding too much of myself, I still find it hard to slow down—my fear of what might happen if I stop is what makes me so driven.

I also block out the fact that I'm no longer capable of working as hard as I once did, ignoring the gradual decline of my body. By remaining as active as I was in my younger years, I'm in some ways putting on an act for my own benefit—pretending I have as much energy in my late forties as I did as a young woman. This is made more difficult by the fact that I still have no idea who I'm supposed to be at this age, or who I want to be. Being constantly in action has become second nature for me, and it will probably take an outside force like a serious illness to eventually slow me down. I'm well aware in theory that my body will begin breaking down by sixty at the latest, but my self-image seems to be simply incapable of incorporating the idea of myself as someone who is aging. By powering through as usual, I push the moment when I will have to ease up as far as possible into the future. But the day will come when the brakes will be abruptly put on for me. It would surely be better for me to try to devise a softer transition to old age if I can; I could slowly begin putting my trust in others to handle my problems, for example, instead of always taking everything into my own hands. For my compulsion to take on responsibilities also prevents anything unplanned or surprising from occurring in my life. Instead of making efforts to market my books myself, for instance, I could simply wait to see what happens if I do nothing; by loosening my grip on such things and letting them run their course, there would be more space in my life for positive developments that I might be preventing with my eternal pushing.

But since I fear that decreased initiative on my part might mean that nothing happens at all, I can't accept the risks that adopting a more passive attitude would bring. Not yet.

    Experience has also taught me there's a strong likelihood my books will be ignored completely, if I myself don't make sure they're spoken about. While this might seem paranoid, it sometimes really does feel as if there's a phobic aversion to my work within Germany. Male reviewers especially often find (indirect) ways of letting me know that what I do is somehow too much; I get the impression that they're unwilling to engage with my literary experiments, on top of my work as an art theorist. As a result, any new publication of mine is treated as incidental or as if it doesn't exist at all. When I visit Antoine in New York, by contrast, I experience the exact opposite: Those I meet express a great interest in my work, and I'm bestowed with recognition and thoughtful words of encouragement. Antoine, especially, constantly promotes my books and work in general, offering me his encouragement like a motivational coach. There are times when his enthusiasm seems excessive, however—I'm not as amazing as he claims. While I appreciate his unconditional support for everything I do, it ultimately doesn't help me; there are naturally valid criticisms to be made of my work, which I would benefit from. But since I'm largely denied a similarly positive level of appreciation in Berlin, I eagerly soak up his pep talks, in spite of everything. The kindness my New York colleagues show toward me is also a balm for the soul. It's astonishing to realize that they respect and value my work; unlike in

Berlin, my status as a woman in a male-dominated art world doesn't seem to have any negative impact on how I'm seen over there. I ask myself whether this might be due to the fact that my style of writing falls between two stools in Germany, or if women in general just receive less encouragement from their male colleagues here. Most likely it's both. Even when I do receive the occasional positive response, I'm suspicious of the compliment: Isn't the applause coming from the wrong side? In any case, the lack of recognition I've experienced in recent years means I now foster an exaggerated skepticism toward my own texts, expecting someone to attack and chastise me for my shortcomings with each essay I publish. Worst of all, though, is to be passed over in silence—when my counterpart doesn't mention my new publication at all. In such moments, it always feels as if I'd been erased, annihilated. That my hunger for acknowledgment is so pronounced is not only due to this lack of professional recognition (which intellectual women in patriarchal societies have dealt with for centuries), however, since the deep pain I feel when I'm ignored in this way also goes back to my childhood. Even as a young girl, I wasn't "recognized" or "seen" by my parents, who were too occupied with themselves to notice me. While good grades were rewarded with a five-mark coin, they had no interest in what I was going through emotionally—there was no place for my actual self in our interactions. And the harder I fought for their acknowledgment, vainly trying to force a positive reaction from them, the greater my fear of disappearing became. My experience was similar in some ways to Klein's description of the small child from whom the "nurturing breast" is withheld (for her, this breast does not necessarily represent the "mother," but other object relations too). Klein argues that the repeated withdrawal of the breast causes the child to develop "persecutive" fears that they can only manage by separating the "bad" (i.e., absent) breast from the mother. From that point on, the child relates to objects as either purely "good" or purely "bad," with no room for nuance or ambivalence. In describing this delusional type of object relation, Klein coined the term "paranoid-schizoid position"—a position that, according to her, we all repeatedly adopt to varying degrees throughout the course of our lives. As soon as we feel threatened, for example, we tend to release the inner pressure we feel by projecting it onto supposedly "bad" objects outside of ourselves. I find this argument fairly persuasive; my perception that I'm constantly confronted with rejection in Germany might also be evidence of me slipping into such a paranoid-schizoid state. Should someone—like myself—lack attention and recognition in childhood (or even adult life), they tend to see a "bad breast," whereas things, in reality, are more complicated. And "more complicated," in my case, means that the absence of any comments about my work does not necessarily equal a rejection of it—it's entirely possible for someone to say nothing about my books while also having read and enjoyed them, after all. But the fear of not being seen, and of disappearing, needs an outlet, and so I get caught up in the (exaggerated) idea that the outside world is hostile toward me. At the same time, there's plenty out there for this paranoid-schizoid worldview to feed on. There are situations in which such a perspective seems entirely appropriate, such as when I am actually disrespected or badly treated by others. But the paranoid-schizoid worldview is always delusional and shot through with massive projections, even if our perceptions of others invariably involve a degree of projection. If we are to avoid becoming paranoid, Klein claims, it can be helpful to compare the delusional images we hold of others with the people themselves. While this is easier said than done, I nonetheless resolve to develop a more realistic image of Antoine. With Klein's help, I've come to understand that it's normal for my "object relations" (that is, my relationships to other people) to be shaped by my anxieties, since according to her, these anxieties are rooted in fears of abandonment and destruction from early childhood. In other words, the massive fear of abandonment I feel regarding Antoine is totally normal. The image I have of him has also been shaped by my anxieties, since fantasies, as Klein writes, *represent* our drives and with this, too, our fears. Fantasies are thus imaginary images in which our fears resonate. And this is also true of the phantasmatic image I have formed of Antoine: Above all, he is a product of my anxieties.

    I resolve to work on cultivating more realistic object relations in the future, and to make them less dependent on paranoid projection. At the same time, I do often experience the fact that certain people don't have my best interests at heart. Perhaps I should show more understanding for their own paranoid-schizoid positions and realize that they're only letting out their inner pressure when they react aggressively or defensively to me. To respond with more empathy to their aggressions would be a good thing, particularly since I'm not free of such aggressions myself. Wouldn't it be better to admit the hostility that rages within me, instead of acting as if I only ever want the best for others? To see oneself as a purely benevolent and good person seems to me to be far more violent. Those who are entirely unaware of what lurks in the depths of their psyche have a sort of uncanny quality for me: Their failure to recognize their own destructive impulses often goes hand in hand with an inflated sense of self-righteousness, which I find hard to bear.

My phone rings. It's Antoine, whose slightly slurred words suggest he might have been drinking. I refrain from making a snippy remark and act as if I hadn't noticed. Full of enthusiasm, he tells me about a dinner he just had with work colleagues and its incredibly collegiate atmosphere. They're now about to head to a bar to continue the party. He tells me how happy he is about the working environment at his firm, where they all stick together despite actually being in competition with one another. It's a lot of fun working under these conditions, he says, and he gets on really well with his colleagues. Biting my tongue, I resist the urge to ask who else is going to the bar, and if there are any women there. Instead, I tell him how happy I am for him, which is also true—in part, at least. I keep the panic his euphoric account of the evening triggers in me to myself, playing the role of the placid and trusting girlfriend while alarm bells ring inside me. My heart races. While I briefly consider being honest with him about my feelings, I know this isn't the right moment. He's drunk, and so he's already slightly detached from the reality my confession would confront him with; to admit my fear of abandonment now would surely only drive him further away from me. But I'm unable to hold it in, and as our conversation comes to an end, I find myself asking if he's been drinking, which he confirms. His admission stings, since he practically never drinks in my company. Does this mean he suppresses his desire to drink when he's with me, and that he only ever really has fun when I'm not there with him? The line suddenly goes dead. He writes me a text message: The connection is really bad, but he hopes I have a nice evening. His reference to the supposedly bad network coverage in New York gives me the impression he's trying to get rid of me— it's a trick we've all seen in one Netflix series or another. I reply that the connection was totally fine, then call him back, but it goes straight to voicemail; he's probably turned his phone off, relieved that I'm no longer able to interrogate him. This sends me into a frenzy, and I call him several times in a row, cursing him for making me humiliate myself in this way. I imagine him turning his attention back to one of his New York flirts while also telling myself that anxiety fantasies of this sort are pure speculation. I have to stop this!

 I already despise myself for not being honest with Antoine about who I really am; he has no idea he's dealing with a psychotic wreck who's plagued by her fears of losing him. Isn't it bad for our relationship for me to pretend to be someone I'm not? In truth, it would be helpful for me to be honest with him about my feelings. But for that I would need to feel secure, and to really trust him.

We're not there yet. One day I will be open with him and tell him about my anxieties, which actually have less to do with him than they do with me. And if he's unable to handle my confession, then he isn't the right man for me. I can hardly wait to arrange this "moment of truth" with him—ideally to be held face-to-face.

    I already know the coming night will be torture. Time and again, I'll wake up and imagine what's happening at that moment in New York. And as soon as the time difference allows—1 p.m. my time, 8 a.m. in New York—I'll wearily call him again. But instead of letting him know how I'm really feeling, I'll just casually ask how his evening was, as I always do. Thankfully I have plans to meet my friend Anne for dinner soon, which will distract me for a few hours at least. The later this awful night begins, the better.

I meet Anne at our regular Italian restaurant. She's brought me flowers—"consolation flowers," she calls them—and they're white tulips, my favorite. I'm touched by her thoughtfulness—all the more so since I do actually need consolation, and this wonderful bouquet of flowers is the most beautiful and encouraging sight I could imagine right now. We spoke on the phone several times before meeting. Anne knows about my problems sleeping, and about my anxieties regarding Antoine. She understands me well; she's had trouble sleeping herself since childhood, and she still lies awake in bed each night. Insomnia is thus her constant companion, and the fact that we both have problems sleeping connects us to one another.

    Even though Anne is always totally exhausted in the morning, she's still enormously productive in her career.

Today, for the first time, she tells me of the financial problems that are plaguing her despite all her successes. Inflation has forced her to drastically reduce her restaurant visits, and she now only takes one holiday every two years, since flights and hotels have almost doubled in price. I feel her pain. My budget, too, has been shrunk by inflation, and in a way, I'm relieved that I'm not the only one experiencing this. Seeing our own fears mirrored in those of the other relativizes them; realizing the other person is going through the same thing as ourselves makes it easier to bear. A problem shared really is a problem halved—we're even able to laugh about our misery together. Moreover, the fact that we're going through something similar actually strengthens the bond between us. Falling into panic at night always make me feel as if I were totally alone in facing the demands of life, isolated by my problems. And yet the opposite is true: My fears actually connect me to others. Together, we form a community of the anxious.

    I make my way home with a spring in my step, humming Justus Köhncke's "Du bist nicht allein"—"You are not alone." I feel at ease, enjoying the moment. Peter, my meditation guide, is right when he says that freeing ourselves from anxiety means being grounded in the present. Fear carries us away into an uncertain future, he says, but by really engaging with what is happening here and now, we realize that this fear is unfounded. While I see some truth in this, the present can also be frightening. My meeting with Anne might have relieved me of some of my more acute fears, but making my way home alone in the dark, I can already feel myself slipping back into some of my other familiar anxious behaviors, such as speeding up and crossing the street when someone is walking behind me. Will fear always catch up with me, then, even in my happier moments?

I just arrived home from the bar; it's now 2 a.m. I lie down in bed and meditate for a while before turning off the light. While I'm still worried by the thought of what Antoine might be up to, I feel relatively relaxed. But it's not long until the next wave of fear hits me, striking me to the core. I'm now extremely tense. I couldn't say exactly what it is I'm afraid of at this moment, but I'm wide awake and on full alert. I know from experience that there's no cure for this feeling, and that herbal sleep tea or valerian tablets won't really help. I'm damned to lie here awake. I try to calm down by telling myself that even if Antoine is getting involved with someone else, then that's OK. There's nothing I can do about it anyway. But trying to fight this impenetrable anxiety with rational observations gets me nowhere; it has me firmly in its grip, spreading throughout my body. I start to feel very hot, which makes sleep even harder. Only a carefree existence could spare me these sorts of nights of horror—a stable life with a solid and present partner and no financial problems. But it quickly dawns on me that no such life exists, without external irritations, injuries, frustrations, humiliations, disappointments, and conflicts. I think of Freud, who declared our interactions with other people to be a central source of our unhappiness, alongside bodily decay and natural catastrophes. Above all, then, it is our relationships with others that lie at the root of our suffering.

That the pain these relationships trigger in us is so great is partly due to the fact that we are unable to control the behavior of those involved; to a certain degree, we're at the mercy of the pains others inflict upon us. There are people who stoically endure these betrayals or deceptions without letting them disturb their inner peace, while others instantly take every hostile remark to heart and spend hours awake thinking about it. I clearly belong to the latter group.

I pick up a book titled *Fear in Capitalism*. It's comforting to immerse myself in the social dimension of my fears, and to realize that the enormous pressure this system puts on people causes most of us to develop anxieties. Weariness overcomes me at some point, and I drift off into a restless sleep. I wake up early the next morning, as I always do during times of emotional turmoil. I realize I was woken by the noise of a passing tram, whose jerks and tremors reverberate through the whole building. There's usually no tramline running through my street, but it's been diverted here during construction work. The tram is so loud that I can even hear it in my bedroom, which looks out onto the inner courtyard of my apartment building. Instantly wide awake, I reach for my phone in panic and check the Twitter page of Berlin's public transport authority. Is this just a temporary diversion due to a demonstration or some other event, or am I facing a long-term disruption due to a construction site somewhere that will persist for months on end? I find the answer I'm looking for: The tram is to be diverted through my street "until further notice." Reading this sends shivers of fear down my spine, since announcements like these usually specify a date when the madness will end. "Until further notice" could mean I'm unable to work in my study for an indefinite period of time; I certainly won't be able to concentrate with a loud, rattling monstrosity shaking my desk at regular intervals. I'm particularly disturbed by the penetrating noise of the tram's bell, which rings out whenever it brakes or approaches the tram stop, tearing me out of my thoughts and making me positively livid.

    I grab my computer and move to the living room, where I set up a temporary workspace. But even here I can hear the dark rumbling of the tram every minute or so, if I prick my ears. It feels as if I've been physically attacked—as if my bodily integrity had been completely disregarded. I wish I were less sensitive to noise. Could the fact that my aversion to it has grown over the years be down to the nature of my work? After all, it's striking that it's often writers like me who feel genuinely threatened by noise—Proust retreated to his cork-lined room to write, while Kafka changed apartments, only to resignedly observe in a letter to Felice that he could still hear his new neighbors even when they whispered.
In my case, I've developed a phobia of the ugly yellow trams that connect the former East of the city, shooting them hateful glances whenever they ride past me. Like aggressive caterpillars, they mercilessly roll toward me, threatening to squash me against the curb if I don't give way. The excessive noise the trams in Berlin produce seems to me to be down to the ancient, squeaky tracks; other cities have long had far more elegant trams, which glide past you with barely a sound. The aversion I've

developed toward Berlin's trams is also connected to the proxy role they play for me: Just as I would slam my bedroom door firmly behind me as a child to discourage my parents from disturbing me while I wrote in my diary, I now escape the tram noises invading my workspace by entrenching myself in my living room. Had my family respected the fact that I was doing something important back then, instead of constantly interrupting me to remind me of familial responsibilities like shared meals and visits, I might not feel so threatened by trams today. But I'm used to pushing through with my work projects against all odds, and so I ward off the sound of the trams like I once did my family from storming into my room and keeping me from writing.

It's not just the noise of the trams that drives me crazy, incidentally; the poor sound insulation in prewar apartment buildings like mine means the loud voices or footsteps of my neighbors also drive me to despair. If I see a moving van parked out front, then I immediately fear the worst, imagining new neighbors who will probably hold constant parties, or whose children will spend every night screaming at each other and gaming. This has been exacerbated by a further disruption in the past week: The neighbors below me have acquired a dachshund, a hunting dog that requires a lot of exercise. This dog barks and yowls all day long, since the family leaves the apartment together at eight o'clock each morning and locks the dog in alone for the rest of the day. This situation is intolerable in two respects: Not only does the dog's constant barking, howling, and whimpering rob me of my concentration, but I also feel sorry for it. In my view, leaving an animal alone for so long is tantamount to cruelty. I politely asked my neighbor to find a solution for this problem when the situation began. Then, when the barking failed to stop, I threatened to demand a rent reduction, which would have been my right given the constant noise. It's now gotten to the stage where my neighbors no longer even respond to my emails when I complain. I even consulted a lawyer, who recommended I compile a "logbook" of the dog's barking. Since then, every bark and yowl has been carefully recorded in this notebook, which lies within arm's reach on my desk at all times. Unfortunately, I've also developed a downright hatred of this dog, despite it bearing no responsibility at all for being neglected and abandoned by its owners. At the beginning of this doggy drama, when my neighbors were still speaking to me, they told me they were considering a brutal technique for disciplining the animal: a specially designed collar that would administer electric shocks to it if it barked. Appalled at this suggestion, I offered to take the dog myself during the daytime instead. They never took me up on my offer, however, and I can no longer imagine looking after this dog all day. My neighbors also turned the tables on me, claiming I'm really the problem for constantly complaining; it's not *their* fault I work from home, after all. As if me and my study were the problem, and not their dog and its constant barking. In any case, I'm now filled with anxiety by the dog's first howls early each morning, on top of the stress of the tram—just hearing it makes me extremely tense, as if my entire working day were now under threat. Playing my own music has proven at least somewhat effective in drowning out the sounds of the dog, and I now listen to loud techno while working, as if trying to defend my normal everyday life with a protective wall of background noise. Producing your own noise is the most effective remedy against the noise made by others.

I need to go shopping, as my fridge no longer has anything edible in it. For days now, I've been ignoring my mailbox as I pass it in the hall, fearing it might contain further demands from my landlord, or worse. This mailbox has something sinister about it in my imagination, and I often pass by it with a studied nonchalance, hoping to escape its evil gaze. I can't bring myself to deal with my mail every single day, since I'm too afraid I might find something that throws me off balance and plunges me into a deep crisis. After returning from the supermarket, however, I gather all my courage. There might be important bills in there that urgently need paying. Opening the mailbox causes a stack of threatening-looking envelopes to fall down on me, which I instantly inspect. One is from my tax adviser's office, informing me of a further payment I need to make. I'm still processing the shock of this when I come across the thing I fear most: a letter from my landlord. Following the rent increase last year, he now wants another—moving forward, I'm supposed to pay him a hundred euros more every month. Since I signed an index-linked rental contract, the local rent cap doesn't apply, meaning he can charge what he wants. My landlord—a notary by trade—is clearly a man with a love of money. While he owns several buildings and has long been a multimillionaire, he seems intent on squeezing ever more rent out of his tenants.

I've developed an aversion to this man; I'm ashamed to admit I've even wished for his death at times. I've never felt so much at someone's mercy as I do with him. My home is his to do with as he wants. I return to my apartment with shaking hands. While the tax payment is bad enough news on its own, having to pay this rent increase every month on top of everything else would simply be beyond my means. I take a deep breath, and in my distress, I decide to call Antoine to tell him of my troubles. That's the point of relationships, after all: to support and console each other in times of crisis. Thankfully he answers, and he patiently listens to me recount my problems. He then suggests lending me money, which I refuse; I'd rather take out a loan than make myself financially dependent on him. At some point our conversation moves on to other subjects, and I mention our shared holiday plans. While we had wanted to spend the summer months together in Germany, he tells me out of nowhere that what had been planned to be two months will now unfortunately only be two weeks—he's too busy at work to allow himself any more than this at the moment; he hopes I understand. I feel stunned, sad, and furious all at once. Once again, he's overturned our plans together, putting his commitments in New York above our relationship and prioritizing his work above all else. And now he expects me to understand and accept this. He abruptly left me alone last winter, despite the fact that my father had fallen seriously sick the day before, and I needed his emotional support. The morning after

I learned of my father's dangerous lung infection, Antoine took his flight as if nothing had happened—staying longer in Berlin for my sake didn't seem to be a consideration for him. There's always something pulling him away from me; he's clearly not prepared to make any concessions to our relationship, and he only fits me into his life when it suits him. I feel a rage and a loneliness rising within me, and in the heat of the moment, I tell him I can't go on like this; I have to cut things off between us. Listening to myself end our relationship, I can barely believe my own words. Is this my unconscious speaking—my anxious self, who can no longer bear all the negative feelings he causes in me? I don't actually want to split up with him at all! Antoine seems as perplexed as I am. "So you're breaking up with me on the phone?" he asks in disbelief. But then he tries to end the call as quickly as possible. He doesn't want to hear from me in the future, he says; it would be too painful for him. And then he's gone. I sit at my kitchen table, numb. I've ended things with my lover without even wanting to. I console myself with the thought that he'll regret our separation—that he'll come back and beg me to give things with him another chance. No doubt about that. And when we've reconciled, he'll visit me far more often in Germany than he did. We needed this break so that we could negotiate the terms of our relationship anew; otherwise, things would have just continued as they were, until he eventually stopped making time for me at all.

I'm too agitated to think about working. Thankfully I'm invited to a dinner this evening. But what should I do with myself until then? I begin by forwarding the letter from my landlord to a lawyer specializing in rental law, in the hope there might be some legal avenue against this new rent rise. Then I look online for videos on fighting financial anxiety. The majority of meditation guides specializing in financial or career anxieties are from the US, and their recommendations always have the same tenor: You simply have to repeat affirmative phrases like "Money comes to me" or "I am abundance," and prosperity will follow. The keyword here is "manifestation"—by stating that "Money will flow to me," my words and thoughts have the power to attract it. By making such a pronouncement, then, we mentally invoke a situation that makes it easier for money to find its way to us. The idea that you can positively influence your financial situation with nothing but the power of thought is magical thinking, of course, since these "manifestations" ignore the fact that there are structural reasons for the financial misery we suffer—numerous studies have been published in recent years proving that the only people wealth flows to these days are those who already have assets and make their money work for itself. To become wealthy through returns from labor alone is no longer possible; on the contrary, the negative impact of inflation on our money means we're getting ever poorer. Nor can the gas levy the German government is currently considering imposing on all citizens simply be conjured away—repeating the mantra that you're swimming in money doesn't make it any truer. At the same time, the belief in the power of these mantras does contain an element of truth—namely, that those who go through life without being tormented by financial anxieties radiate a different aura than those who have to count every cent. Moreover, anyone who optimistically assumes the money they desire will flow toward them at some point exudes a sense of confidence that improves their chances of this actually happening—at least in my experience.

I attempted to give my belief in my own abundance a boost yesterday, by paying the check for a very expensive meal with a friend. Allowing myself this gesture of generosity was frightening, given the current state of my bank balance; I went beyond my means the moment I even picked out the overpriced restaurant. But I told myself that, by simulating wealth, the money I threw away on the meal would reappear somehow. There's been no sign of this yet, however. The word "abundance" makes me think of Antoine, who's financially secure and lives like a king over in New York. While I always give the impression that I'm determined to be financially independent, I secretly long for someone who will take me in and protect me if I ever need it. Antoine could have been this person; he could have offered me the financial security I crave—and I just let him go. Have I gone mad?

I wish I could use alcohol to numb the deep pain I feel from this separation, like others in my circle do in such situations, but I don't drink or keep any alcohol at home. When someone offered me a glass of champagne recently, I took a few quick sips, and even this was enough to lift my spirits: I felt less burdened by life, as if anything were possible. My tongue loosened by alcohol, I also became more outspoken, saying things I would usually keep to myself at any cost and on the verge of holding a long-winded and overly personal monologue. My usual anxious attitude toward life was replaced by a feeling of omnipotence—not only did I become increasingly talkative, but I also felt braver and more self-confident. Had I carried on drinking, I would have eventually reached a state of fearless disinhibition. But I also know from my friends who do drink alcohol regularly that its effects are only temporary, and that the anxiety it chases away returns the next day in all its fury. While the option of being free of this anxiety for even just an evening seems like a seductive one, my problem is that I simply don't enjoy the taste of alcohol—I find beer downright disgusting, and wine is too bitter for me. I have to force myself to consume either. The only way I can enjoy alcohol is in sweet drinks; it's like my tastes haven't changed since childhood. This is compounded by the fact that excessive enjoyment of alcohol goes against my mania for control: If I do take a few sips, my self-defense mechanism kicks in the moment I sense myself getting even a little carried away. My inability to let myself go makes me an unsuitable candidate for drinking. For me, there's nothing harder than "letting go," as we're now so often demanded to do. I'm afraid to put myself at the mercy of others, and so I avoid alcohol, which can have just that effect. And yet my abstinence also seems to have the benefit that I always have a clear head, unlike the drinkers in my circle. I'm often the only one who can still remember what happened the night before the next morning. But for this, I miss out on certain intense and transgressive experiences, which I regret.

I sit down at my desk to continue working on my book on the specific value-form of the artwork. I've been making slow progress for weeks now—it feels as if I were operating in a vacuum with my observations on value, since it's essentially not a topic of much interest to anyone else in the field. I should talk to others more about my ideas, instead of working away on my own all the time; the more isolated I am in pursuing my research, the more irrelevant it seems. What purpose is theorizing and defining the particular value-form of artistic work even supposed to serve, exactly?

I tell myself that I shouldn't be disheartened by a lack of response to my work; I need to learn to trust myself more, and to develop a sense of my own self-worth that's less reliant on the validation of others. But it's hard to satisfy this hunger when, like me, you define yourself through writing, which fundamentally aims for recognition. I want to be acknowledged and heard, even if I don't have a specific audience in mind while I'm writing. And although writing, for me, is a form of self-conversation, it also inherently addresses an outside, like all language. Writing is a solitary process, but it's done in the hope that the text will reach like-minded individuals who, the author hopes, will see themselves reflected in it. To free oneself entirely from the desire for a response from readers is thus impossible for a writer.

For me, my imagined audience also takes on the function of a superego that makes relentlessly strict demands of me and insists on high standards. This brings me back to Klein, who interestingly relates the superego to the fear of death. More precisely, she claims that the fear of death is actually the "descendant" of the fear of the superego, meaning we see our superego as posing a similar threat to us as death itself. The commands my superego issues to me often resonate with my anxieties, such as my fear of not meeting my own (entirely excessive) standards. It announces itself as an inner voice, which implores me to "try harder and do better." It tells me to be more resolute in pursuing my projects, and to take care of marketing books myself as much as possible. My superego is a merciless taskmaster. The commands this inner drill sergeant issues me reflect all the societal ideals I've largely internalized in spite of my criticism of them, like the imperative for hard work and personal responsibility. While I see a healthy work-life balance as something worth aspiring to in principle, that's far from saying I actually organize my everyday life along those lines. Instead, I listen to the voice of my superego, which warns me not to stand still—something I'd be unable to afford anyway. The older and closer to death I get, the harder it is to ignore its messages: The clock is ticking, and every minute counts. It's precisely because my time is getting increasingly scarce as I approach fifty that my mania for work and hyperactivity have taken on entirely new dimensions. Is this the despairing energy of the late career, a sort of final surge before my body forces me to slow down? Friends of mine, most of them younger than me, have recently found more and less subtle ways of reminding me I'll be reaching pension age before too long, which sounds to me as if they're secretly hoping I'll soon step back and finally give them all some peace. I generally ignore such comments. "If only you knew what's inside me," I secretly think to myself, "about all the plans I still have, and the demons driving me to work harder! You might think you've seen everything I have to offer, but that's nothing compared to what's coming!"

It's time to get changed for dinner. I shouldn't actually be subjecting myself to social situations in this state, since I know from experience that following through on such commitments when I'm in bad shape carries heavy risks—others might sense my vulnerability and seize the opportunity to humiliate me with their pointed remarks. I can only enter the stage of the art world when I'm armed with the right equipment—that is, when I'm able to play along with this charade in which everyone acts as if their lives are going perfectly. At the very least, I need the right outfit, to protect me from potential attacks from outside like a suit of armor. So, what should I wear? I settle on a black jacket with wide shoulders, jeans, a white shirt, and high-heeled boots. This has become my go-to ensemble for crisis situations, lending me a sense of confidence even when I'm actually at the end of my rope. The dinner is organized by the art collector Sabine Morat, a rich heiress who only emerged in the art world a few years ago. No one took her seriously at first, but her standing grows with every artwork she buys. Like other collectors before her, she had to endure humiliating initiation rituals before being accepted into the fold, after which she was treated as if she'd always belonged there.

She's now actively courted by most members of the art world, in the hope that she'll buy something from them or lend them her support somehow. Speak to her for any sustained period of time, however, and you clearly sense the insecurity of someone who doesn't actually know much about art and relies on advisers to make her decisions. Her worry that others might only like her for her money is also written all over her face. She's always at the forefront of fashion, wearing pieces from the latest collections by the hippest designers. She can easily afford these expensive items—she recently paired a Balenciaga dress with a Celine handbag, for example—and expensive dermatological treatments have halted the usually inexorable process of aging. She now looks far better than she did in her younger years—her skin ironed smooth, her nose narrower, her lips fuller. Looking at Morat, it's clear that it's ultimately a question of money whether a woman is visibly aging or not. While anyone who can't afford regular injections of Botox and hyaluronic acid develops frown lines on their forehead that become deeper over time, eventually making them look tired and permanently angry, Morat has erased the traces of aging and still looks like a young girl, despite being well over fifty. Beyond this, she's also a good example of the fluctuations and conjunctural shifts of the art world, where someone looked down on by all can quickly become universally loved.

    I set off to her showroom, where I take a quick look at the exhibition (mostly uninteresting, in my view) before hurrying on to the restaurant. A diagram of the seating arrangement hangs on the wall, and the guests huddle in front of it, curious to see who they'll be spending the evening sitting next to. I've been placed between a curator and a gallery employee, as if ensuring that those with less money and more intellectual capital stay among themselves. The collector herself is seated at the most "important" table, directly next to the artist whose works are on display in the showroom and surrounded by the gallerists and other powerful collectors. The table is protected by an invisible cordon sanitaire—a palpable barrier ensuring those sitting behind it are kept apart from the rest of us. While other guests can glance over and follow what is happening, Queen Morat admits no one else to this central table, preventing anyone without money from coming into contact with the financial elite. The danger of this social order becoming unsettled is thus averted, leaving no possibility for advancement to a higher sphere.

I resolve not to tell my neighbors at the table anything about my private misery; beyond the fact that I barely know them, to speak of my drama with Antoine would only reactivate the pain I feel at losing him. In need of some distraction, I talk to the curator about exhibitions, artists, and books we're currently reading while the gallery employee complains about her working conditions and low pay. I feel repeated pangs of pain during our conversation—a reminder that I'm actually unhappy—and I ask myself if others can see what I'm really going through. The meal stretches on forever, with the main course served at 11 p.m. The thought that I'll soon be returning to my apartment alone makes my stomach cramp up. The strict seating arrangement has loosened up a little by now, with a few guests circulating and fighting for better seats by seeking out conversations with "more important" people at other tables. The mood is becoming more and more exuberant; some guests are slightly drunk, and the social barriers between them seem increasingly surmountable—even those at the bottom of the art world hierarchy are now suddenly finding themselves in conversation with rich collectors. The mere sight of all this activity makes me feel instantly exhausted. I need to get home as quickly as possible; trying to read my own current market value based on others' gazes is too exhausting. Some of the people I speak to find subtle ways of signaling to me that critics like me are less in demand than we used to be. We're now mostly seen as an irritation—as killjoys who poison the well by raising unnecessary objections to things the majority of the art world approves of. Or am I just imagining this drop in status? While some people in the art world do actually appreciate my work, my symbolic capital carries less weight than the bank balances of potential buyers and collectors. My role within this system is that of a user who tries to steer a tiny proportion of the monetary value circulating within it into her own pocket. Art world transactions are essentially based on the premise that critics will load artworks with meaning for almost no reward. And while the enormous profits made by successful artists and gallerists are also partly due to the work critics do in producing meaning, it's an unwritten rule that the latter only receive a small share of the takings. Despite this, I sometimes feel like a parasite within this scene, since my work is ultimately subordinated to that of the artists themselves. Or are these just the depressed thoughts of a newly single person? I resolve to undo this impulsive breakup once I'm home; it doesn't feel right, and I didn't really want it in the first place.

The door to my apartment building slams shut behind me when I enter. It's been doing this for several days now—a spring must be broken—but of course it hasn't occurred to the property management company to repair it. The mercilessly loud bang of the door also seems to symbolize my pitiless situation. There's no one who could soothe or dampen the pain I'm feeling right now. Nothing to cushion me from it. My only option is to call my now-ex-boyfriend—to tell him I acted in the heat of the moment and that I never wanted to break things off with him at all. But Antoine doesn't answer. Could he even have blocked me?

I consider calling Linda, a mutual friend in New York, to find out from her how he's doing. Has he made our split public already, or is he still keeping it secret? Is he suffering too, or did he quickly resume business as usual? Linda's busy, but she promises to call me back in a few minutes. In the meantime, I make a cup of tea and read the email from my lawyer, who has two recommendations for me. The first is that I have his office check the validity of the index clause in my rental contract, which would cost me €400 an hour. The second is that I measure the floor plan of my apartment and compare this to what's stated in the contract; if it turns out to be smaller, I'll receive a partial refund on the rent I've already paid. I find this all incredibly stressful. I can already see myself crawling around, armed with a tape measure but without really knowing how I'm supposed to take these measurements. A nightmare. I also balk at the thought of paying for my contract to be checked, which would fill my mailbox with invoices that I'm no more able to pay than I am the increased rent. This decision will have to wait until another day.

    Linda calls me back, and her voice sounds strangely hoarse—she's clearly not finding this conversation easy. I tell her how much pain the split with Antoine is causing me, and that I've decided to reverse my decision. Her answer is brief: "Forget about him." Hearing this makes me freeze: Why should I abandon hope and strike him, my great love, from my memory? I dig deeper, pushing her for a reason. After some hesitation, she says simply: "He's seeing someone else." I'm speechless. How can he be dating someone else already? Isn't he mourning the end of our relationship? Linda tells me she saw Antoine yesterday evening with his new girlfriend, who had been "waiting in the wings" for several weeks already; she doesn't want to reveal her name, which she says would be too painful for me. My mind now in a fever, I ask myself who this woman could be, who instantly threw herself at him the moment he was single. I land on Natalie, an artist from Berlin who now lives in New York. She's been single for some time, and I recently observed her ostentatiously flirting with Antoine at an opening. She would be the perfect replacement for me. I end my conversation with Linda and start manically looking for pictures of Natalie online. After scrolling through a selection of her selfies, all taken in sexy poses, I eventually come across a photo of her and Antoine that must have been taken last night. The two of them attended an opening together. Antoine looks into the camera with a slightly embarrassed expression, while Natalie proudly parades her catch. I'm devastated; he managed to replace me in less than twenty-four hours. Instead of wasting time grieving me, he instantly found someone else. I've never felt so worthless. While I know that fixating on my rival and offloading all my rage onto her is wrong, I could kill Natalie, particularly since she seems to have no concept of sisterhood or solidarity among women. But I mustn't let myself forget that Antoine is the real villain in this story—that he was the one who betrayed me and our relationship. On top of this, there's the added social humiliation he's now inflicting on me by demonstrating to the world how well he's getting on without me. My role in his life was merely that of the "girlfriend," whose function can easily be taken over by anyone else.

There'll be no sleep for me tonight. I try calling Antoine, hoping to offload my anger on him, but of course he doesn't answer. Replacing me the way he did has triggered the old and deep-seated pain of the abandoned child. My childhood was shaped by two experiences of being brutally deserted and replaced. When I was around five years old, my mother dropped my sister and me off at a children's home on the island of Norderney, telling us she had to leave us there briefly but would be back soon. We didn't see her again until six weeks later. The period in between was spent suffering at the hands of the children's home's poisonous approach to pedagogy, feeling entirely forlorn and rejected. By the time our mother did eventually pick us up, we felt emotionally alienated from her. My father left the family a few years later to marry a woman twenty years younger than him, with no bedroom for us in his new house. He shut us out of his life, simply moving on without creating any space for us in his new situation. This was made more difficult by the fact that our mother kept the divorce a secret for a long time. She wanted to protect us. Unfortunately, I came across the divorce papers while sitting at her desk one day, and my trust in my mother has never fully recovered.

    I think the lesson to take from this situation with Antoine might be that I need to relive this old pain from my childhood once again, so that I'm better able to integrate it into my psyche. Perhaps him putting me through the thing I fear most—being not just left but replaced—will make it easier for me to deal with my childhood fear of abandonment more calmly. This is little consolation, however. I won't regain my stability without help. I need sleeping tablets or tranquilizers—anything that will pull me out of my state of total desolation. I call Anne, who tells me her own doctor once prescribed her tranquilizers and suggests I visit him with her tomorrow morning. Since tea and meditation are no longer helping, I agree. I repeatedly try to reach Antoine throughout the night, deliberately avoiding leaving him a voicemail so he doesn't have anything he can use against me.

After spending the night awake with my thoughts circling around Antoine and our relationship, Anne picks me up to travel to her doctor together. Through my tears, I tell this stranger about the spiritual and bodily torment I'm suffering, describing my heartbreak using the metaphor of a sword pierced through my body. The doctor asks me how I, an "accomplished woman," could be so totally floored by this separation. How is it possible that my entire sense of well-being is dependent on this man? I try to explain to him that the demands of my professional life mean I need someone to encourage and support me, that I find it hard to fall asleep without hearing a few calming words from my lover, for example. The doctor dryly remarks that it sounds to him as if men were replaceable for me, since their primary function is to support me, which in principle anyone can do. This makes me wonder if I did actually "use" Antoine, just as he probably cast me to play a particular role in his life. He might have sensed that it wasn't him at all that I was really interested in deep down, and so he found someone else instead. I decide that I'll have to get by without the protective and reassuring figure of a boyfriend or partner from now on. In the meantime, though, I need medical support. The doctor gives me some strong sedatives that are supposed to dampen my mood during the day and help me sleep at night. He also suggests I see a therapist. I swallow the first tablets while I'm still in the waiting room, and I soon notice myself slowing down and feeling increasingly drowsy. The medicine creates a numbing film around my body and soul, preventing the pain from getting in. At the same time, it also makes me feel weak and foggy. Once home, I immediately have to lie down, after which I spend hours dozing in bed. I might have succeeded in deadening the piercing pain, but what about my professional commitments, like my deadlines and everything else? Even eating takes painstaking effort in this state; keeping an appointment would take strength I don't have. Anne calls again and expresses her concern at how slowly I'm speaking. She tells me she's coming over right away, and a few minutes later, she's standing at my door. When I go to lie down again, she spiritedly pulls me out of bed. She suggests we ring in my new phase of life "sans boyfriend" by redesigning my apartment. A store I know in Charlottenburg is having a massive sale at the moment, so we could potentially buy a few pieces of furniture. I stagger along to her car with her, and we drive there together so I can pick out a new sofa and coffee table. While I don't actually have the money for such purchases, I decide to max out my overdraft for this symbolic fresh start. It's worth it. My apartment will be a different one, and I'll drive the memory of Antoine out of it—from now on, it will be mine alone. I have to stop with the tablets, though; living in this deadened and emotionless state scares me. On the way home, we run into an old acquaintance of mine—Gerald—on the street. When he casually asks how I am, I burst into tears and tell him of my heartache. I suddenly realize that, with the loss of Antoine, my prospects of a different and possibly better life have also disappeared. He was the first man I might have been able to imagine having a family with one day. While it's probably too late for that already, I haven't started menopause yet, so I'm still fertile—things might have worked out. Gerald is visibly shocked by my desolate state and offers to let me stay at his house on Gran Canaria for a few weeks while I recover. He's traveling there himself next month and says

I'm welcome to come along; there's a separate bedroom and study there I can use. The mere thought of the beach and the ocean pulls me out of my misery. I'm positively elated at his suggestion—the ocean has always had a healing effect on me, freeing me from my love-life drama and feelings of jealousy. I picture us working there each day and setting off to the beach together. And how I will be regenerated.

Tonight, though, I still have to fulfill a commitment I made long ago, when I agreed to appear at a roundtable discussion on the topic of "Aesthetic Judgment in the Post-Medium Era." Thankfully I have something up my sleeve—a short contribution titled "Like and Subscribe" that considers how artworks should be judged. I go through the text one more time, reading it aloud and underlining the parts to be emphasized. Acting professionally will do me good. Even in my greatest crisis, I need only flick a mental switch, and I can perform in public with such confidence that no one would guess how desolate I'm really feeling. I pull on the black jacket with the slightly padded shoulders and set off to the event; it's always a good idea to wear something padded when on a panel with men, as they usually take up a lot of space and extending myself in this way helps me claim more of it for myself. When I arrive, twenty minutes before the event is due to start, I note with alarm that almost no one has come. The embarrassed faces of the organizers and my fellow participants stare back at me from rows of empty chairs—not even our friends and acquaintances seem to have made it. The event was announced through all the usual channels, as far as I know; perhaps, as so often in Berlin, something more important is going on somewhere else? I feel as if I've been abandoned. This is often the case with such events, unfortunately: I picture myself delivering my talk to the "right audience" beforehand, imagining halls full of people all interested in what I have to say, but the reality often looks quite different, and barely anyone turns up. While close friends might be expected to come and sit in the front row out of solidarity, even they stay away; people have other commitments, after all, and there's simply too much for them to do anyway. Turning to the organizers, I remark that it's not exactly full. They claim to be surprised by this themselves, particularly since there were numerous bookings made in advance. The participants take their places, and I deliver my keynote speech to empty seats. Thankfully the discussion goes very well despite this, and I resolve to enjoy this clandestine gathering; there are even some appreciative and productive questions from the audience at the end of our conversation. The discussion is followed by a dinner, during which I tell a colleague of my attempt to banish the aura of my ex-boyfriend with a new sofa and coffee table. When she asks what I'm planning to do with the old sofa, I offer to give it to her for free, since I know she often has financial difficulties and want to do her a favor. She's delighted by my suggestion, and we arrange for the sofa to be picked up the following morning.

I slept better last night, thankfully, and I managed to keep my misery about Antoine at bay. My early appointment means I have to shower as soon as I wake up, which does me good. My friend arrives with her brother, and the three of us heave the bulky sofa into the elevator; we have to remove the feet from it before it can be loaded into the van, which blocks the elevator for a few minutes. My landlord then appears out of nowhere, having stormed up the stairs, his face red with strain. He screams at me that the elevator is *for people only*, and that using it for anything else is strictly forbidden; he wanted to take it up to his penthouse, and now we've forced him to use the stairs. He pants with exertion while he berates us. I repeatedly apologize, explaining the situation to him, and we move the sofa as quickly as we can. A few hours later, after summoning the courage to empty my mailbox, I find a handwritten warning letter from my landlord. He must have written and deposited it immediately after our unhappy encounter. Panicked at the thought that my contract might now be terminated, I take a photo and send it to my lawyer. My home is under threat again.

 The issue of how my work is received in public also continues to occupy me. Even when people do come in numbers, there can be problems. There are often times when I fail to create a connection with the audience, for example, which I usually realize before I've even finished speaking. I've thus repeatedly resolved to take a freer and more confident approach to my readings. This is easier said than done, however: If there are certain people in the audience whose presence makes me nervous, for example, or if I register that not everyone is reacting positively, then I find it hard to deviate from the script

I've prepared. I now realize I failed to make a good impression at yesterday's event too. I was tense. As a result, I spent my journey home being tortured by the questions of what I might have done or phrased differently.

    I was still brooding over this after an afternoon walk, when I opened the door of my apartment building, only to be greeted by the overwhelming stench of dog excrement. The entire hallway was covered with feces, some of which had already been trodden on by my neighbors; even the doormat was full of remnants of dog waste. Reaching the elevator with clean shoes wasn't easy, and I hopped around the filthy areas of the floor while doing my best to hold my breath. What on earth happened? Could it have been my neighbors' wretched dog, sick with diarrhea and relieving itself all over the hallway? For one person to carry so much excrement in on their shoe seems barely possible. Or was it an anonymous protest by some other tenants, signaling their unhappiness at the latest exorbitant rent increase? It's hard to say. While I briefly considered informing the building's management of the desolate state of the entrance hall, it's not in my nature to play the role of janitor. I don't want to be the one constantly pointing out problems and reporting on what's going on in the building; I'd rather endure the stench that is sure to linger in the air and hold my nose when I'm crossing the hallway. To me, this incident seems like a drastic illustration of a wider drop in living standards— the fact that no one (including the management company) is going to take responsibility for cleaning the mess up is symptomatic of the end of the social pact. No longer are such problems seen as something to be overcome collectively; on the contrary, we're now expected to deal with them alone, and to simply put up with the excrement in the hallway.

I'm listening to Baroque music in the kitchen. As with techno, I highly recommend this music to anyone who, like me, sometimes struggles with anxiety. The rapid tempo creates an instant sense of euphoria, carrying you away with it; a lot of classical music was originally dance music, after all, and I see techno as today's equivalent. I move to the rhythm of Mozart's *An die Freundschaft*, enthusiastically singing the lyrics I still remember from my childhood singing lessons. Listening to "my music" always makes me feel instantly better; even domestic chores like laundry or emptying the dishwasher seem easier when they're accompanied by my favorite melodies. Mozart's aria lifts me out of myself, giving me a renewed sense of purpose and the ability to take some pleasure from a situation that now seems more manageable. At the same time, Teresa Ringholz's voice cuts me to the core, and my eyes fill with tears at the very first note she sings. As someone trained in bel canto singing, her voice has a physicality that makes me feel a tangible connection not just to her but to all people, with all their joys and their pain. Music has the potential to connect the individual with the general, since you're both alone and in company while listening to it.

    I follow Mozart with some techno, dancing wildly around the kitchen to Roland Appel's *Fleurs du mal* and feeling fantastic. I'd love to be able to listen to music all day, as it would leave no room for my anxiety to take hold—I would exist on a "higher" level then, beyond the reach of my worries and fears. Unfortunately, I'm unable to write and listen to music simultaneously, since I'm no multitasker and can only concentrate on one thing at a time. With a heavy heart, I end my invigorating listening session and return to my desk. A penetrating silence dominates, giving my negative thoughts all the room they could want.

Scrolling Instagram, I just discovered another photo of Antoine and Natalie—a freshly enamored couple clearly enjoying their busy social life. To add insult to injury, Natalie is far slimmer than I am; Antoine was probably never really attracted to me, and now he's found his dream woman. I scan the photo for hidden messages. His expression seems furtive somehow—a sign of guilt, perhaps? Is he trying to signal to me that he's unhappy about our separation? Or is this just wishful thinking on my part? I feel a strong urge to know how things are going with his new relationship, and whether he might be secretly missing me. But the fact is that we're no longer together; he might still try to win me back, but this would require him to fly to Berlin. I forbid myself from calling him again, repeating the mantra that he's now with someone else and clearly wants nothing to do with me. I should throw myself back into my own life here in Berlin, instead of torturing myself with these painful online investigations. But it's hard when everything here frightens me at the moment. I ask myself how I'm supposed to manage my life with all its financial and professional problems without Antoine's emotional support. I'll sink without him. The greater my fear of collapse becomes, the harder I find it to be optimistic about my future. I can barely imagine finishing my book on the value of art; I'll certainly never meet the deadline set by the publishers, who wanted it finished by the end of the year. I need inner peace, concentration, and calm for this project, but all I have instead is the pain of separation. Instead of tackling my book, I just sit nervously at my desk, thinking about either Antoine or my financial problems. Of course, my money problems are on the "luxury" end of the spectrum; I have a steady income, after all, which must seem positively gigantic to others. I belong to the much-invoked "middle class," whose diminished social status as a group is now clear for all to see. To this extent, my fears are justified—at the very least, there's a danger of slipping even further. The typical trappings of middle-class life, such as taking holidays or buying an apartment, are no longer affordable for us (while for others they never were, of course).

I often try to banish thoughts of my future, and to focus on the present instead. But time is running out, since the older I get, the harder it becomes for me to change track. I'm actually under permanent pressure. To be able to think properly about the "value of art" would require me to block out all that is currently burdening me—an utter impossibility.

It's curious that few of my friends and acquaintances have received letters informing them of increased rent or utility costs—my landlord seems to be a fast mover. Today is the day of my appointment with the tenants' association, so I make my way to the nearest office, on

Schönhauser Allee, which resembles a run-down station waiting room. I sit down in a white plastic chair in a bare, windowless room whose glaring yellow walls are probably meant to create a sunny mood. Sound carries so well within this space that I can hear the conversations of other tenants seeking advice in the adjoining rooms as people repeatedly shuffle past me with coffee cups on their way to the machine. The staff seem bent with sorrow; the longer I sit here, the more their body language robs me of any hope. I ask myself whether this might be the mark of spending their days vainly fighting the machinations of scheming property owners. On the one hand, every detail in these offices seems designed to put visitors on the defensive—like the lonely plant in the corner, which seems to symbolize the isolation of the individual under capitalism. On the other hand, the tenants' association actually defends its members, by supporting them in their fight against their landlords, in return for a low membership fee. When my name is finally called out, I'm called to a consultation room. The lawyer advising me begins by taking a long swig from a can of Red Bull, as if needing that boost of energy to cope with my misery. He's instantly in top form, however, dictating a highly competent and legally watertight letter to my landlord to me to write down. I'm also supposed to contact him again as soon as my landlord sends me the next bill for my utilities; should it lead to a further rent increase, he'll forward the case to a higher authority who will file a complaint against it as "extortionate." He says I can ignore the "warning" my landlord left in my mailbox about moving the sofa in the elevator, since the corresponding passage in my rental contract is "immoral" under German law. I instantly feel better—finally, someone who's willing to help me. This meeting hasn't really changed anything about my current situation, however, since this lawyer, like my landlord, advises me to put money aside for the building charges, which are sure to rise. But at least it seems possible that he might be able to prevent an exponential increase in the rent itself. He tells me about the tenants' association's lobbying efforts to get the rent cap extended to include index-linked rental contracts, and that various support packages are currently being put together by the state to help German citizens meet the exorbitant heating costs coming their way. Buoyed by this news, I step into the street and immediately stop off at a café. The positive effects of my consultation don't last long, however, and my anxieties return just a few hours later. I'm suddenly struck with fear at the thought that my refusal to pay the increased utility costs might give my landlord legal grounds to evict me; apparently, my anxieties only paused to catch their breath during my meeting, before overwhelming me again without warning.

Having returned home, I'm unable to force myself to work, and so I read online about a much-discussed talk given recently by a fellow writer. Unfortunately, this does nothing to lighten my mood. I'm immediately struck by how dramatically this author addresses his audience, repeatedly raising his arms in the air like a priest preaching to his congregation. His solemn demeanor seems to satisfy his largely male audience's desire for spiritual leadership. And yet the euphoric reports of his talk in the newspapers' arts pages fail to note that the cosmos it invokes is an exclusively male one. Men alone are of significance to this author, and the few women who do get a mention in his work are mercilessly dissed. His male disciples then return his affection by post, by writing eulogies to him in the daily newspapers; this is a world where men celebrate other men, and where women are not to be taken seriously. That women working in the cultural field can still be devalued in this way in the post-#MeToo era makes me feel demoralized and depressed. I ask myself what my own status is in such a misogynistic industry. It's clear that sexist structures are deeply anchored in the social fabric, and it seems to me as if I have to fight the old feminist battles for equality time and again, always starting from scratch. It's so exhausting!

    I call Anne to discuss my impressions of the author's talk with her; she shares my opinion entirely. At some point we move on to talking about what's really tormenting me: my separation from Antoine and the anxieties it has triggered in me. I tell her of my fear of being abandoned and of what might happen in the future. I also tell her about my financial problems. The truth is I now have a permanently queasy feeling in my stomach. Fear has taken root in my body and is making itself known in various ways—my chest feels contracted, and my shoulders and back are painfully tense. I'm a wreck. Anna advises me to give medication another try, arguing that you have to stick with it for it to work. She found a drug that has freed her of her own "lower-level" anxieties and is now able to go through life with less fear. It takes a while for it to take effect, she says; you just have to be patient and keep switching medications until you find the right one. I tell her how numb and incapable of action I felt after taking the sedatives. I don't ever want to feel so paralyzed again. I'm also not looking to chase away my fears; I just want to learn how to deal with them differently, like my meditation guide, Peter, recommends. Perhaps I should actually think about starting therapy. Any sense of optimism disappears once fear has found its way into my consciousness, and I always expect to fail. And as soon as I assume my desires will not be fulfilled—such as landing a lucrative consultant job in the auction sphere, for example—I radiate a sense of hopelessness that inevitably earns me one rejection after another. My fears then seem as if they are all too justified—a vicious cycle that therapy might help me break out of.

    I came across a further technique for managing anxiety in Elfriede Jelinek's play *Angabe der Person* (Personal details). After mentioning how fear "punctually" comes to her each day the moment she rises, she then describes her method of simply imposing this anxiety on other people, who "should see how it feels themselves for once." Like Jelinek, I could try to free myself of my fears by passing them on to others—my readers, for example.

It's time to book my emergency trip to the beach, where I'll spend three weeks staying at Gerald's house. Not being able to assess the spatial situation there makes me nervous—will I have a bathroom to myself, as well as my own bedroom, or will I have to awkwardly traipse through the house each morning before I've even put on my makeup? I also need to find out if his house is on a busy road; I know from experience that traffic noise can be unbearably loud on an island when you're on the coast. This makes me think of Proust and his own sensitivity to noise. His letters to his mother include regular complaints about his living conditions—not just that his rooms were noisy, but even that his hotel bed was placed in the wrong spot yet couldn't be moved. So, Proust also had trouble sleeping. Hopefully such details won't deprive me of my own sleep.

I search for a cheap flight on easyJet, but travel has become significantly more expensive since the pandemic. The more time I spend online, the more furious I become with airlines like easyJet, which now not only demand twice as much money for a ticket but also require their customers' unpaid assistance during the booking process. It takes forever for me to book my flight, baggage, and "speedy boarding" before finally printing out my boarding pass. I wonder if I'll have to battle pre-travel anxiety again before setting off this time, as I have so often recently. I never used to feel this way before traveling—it's only since my anxieties around abandonment, money, and the future have ramped up that I've been suffering mild panic attacks before flying. My anxieties clearly enjoy reproducing themselves.

It's for this reason that I now write packing lists before traveling, to ensure I don't forget anything and am prepared for all eventualities. Even this doesn't help, however: I then picture my suitcase getting lost, forcing me to spend days getting by without my special contact lens solution and cosmetics, in spite of my packing list. I therefore stash the essentials in a small pouch in my hand luggage, just in case. I also imagine a situation in which my bank card suddenly stops working, and so I write down the emergency phone number for my bank and take it with me. Even worse would be the loss of my phone, as then I'd have none of my contacts to hand. Shuddering at the thought, I write a list with the most important numbers. I also picture my computer giving up the ghost—another nightmare scenario. Perhaps I should invest in a backup tablet? To be tortured by anxious visions of this sort before a holiday is new for me. While I used to be extremely relaxed about traveling, trusting that everything would work out and curious to experience new situations, I now need certain conditions to feel comfortable and secure—above all peace and quiet. And since there's no way to verify noise levels in advance, the prospect of experiencing the unfamiliar makes me feel uneasy and anxious.

    I therefore attempt to avert or minimize any potential disasters—from street noise to a lost suitcase—in advance. But as soon as I've found a solution for one problem, another appears; there's simply no end. I think back to my holidays with Antoine, and how secure I felt in his company—his higher standard of living alone took a lot of the stress out of traveling. It really does make a difference what class you travel. Fly economy, and you spend hours standing around at check-in, only to stand around again in an overfilled waiting room before being squeezed in between the other economy passengers at the back of the aircraft. In business class, by contrast, passengers head straight to their own check-in desk— as I did with Antoine—then the lounge, before stretching their legs out during the flight itself. The cabin crew takes your coat for you, serves you a reasonable meal, and generally treats you better throughout. Unfortunately, I can't afford to fly business. Spending the four-hour flight to the Canaries in the cheap seats will be an ordeal. Anyone who's "only" able to fly economy is more at the mercy of the vagaries of travel, as well as their fears. Other sorts of journeys are far more stressful, of course; once again, my complaints are those of the privileged.

My father is currently in Berlin, so we meet for an early dinner at his hotel; he's in the city for work and wants to see me while he's here. I mentioned my troubles with Antoine when we spoke on the phone earlier. He's entirely incapable of dealing with emotions and emotional breakdowns, unfortunately, and so responding to my romantic dramas and life crises in any meaningful way is entirely beyond him. Like many men of his generation, he has no insight into his own emotional life; I've never seen him cry, for example. When I told him of my misery during our phone call, his initial response was one of concerned silence. He eventually forced himself to say he was sorry. I could sense how strongly he hoped my desolate state would soon pass—he finds me easier to deal with when I'm on the sunnier side of life.

    At tonight's dinner, I ask him about *his* marriage; he's been married to my stepmother for twenty-five years already, and I want to know how he's managed to stay with her for so long. (That I myself don't like her is no secret.) "It just turned out that way," he answers evasively.

I realize that he sees his marriage as a fate he has passively submitted himself to. He says nothing of love; for him, their relationship is not something he has actively chosen or shaped but a mere fact that he resignedly accepts. I tell him of my heartbreak, and how sad I am that Antoine got together with another woman just twenty-four hours after our separation. My father tries to console me by telling me that's "just how men are"; they're not capable of being alone, and so they instantly need to find a replacement. He's clearly thinking of himself here, since he, too, secretly remarried just three months after my mother divorced him. I burst into tears, screaming at him in fury: How can he talk about "men" as if they were all the same, when there are plenty of men who do go through a period of mourning after a breakup and manage to stay single for more than a couple of weeks at a time? It's also unhelpful for him to explain Antoine's behavior with a supposed anthropological constant instead of being outraged by it; it almost feels like he's taking Antoine's side instead of supporting me. When he eventually relents, it's in his own inimitably clumsy way: I don't need to worry, he says, I'm attractive and will find someone else. It's hopeless with him. His words of comfort are poisonous, since they suggest I can only be loved for how I look. Appearances were always important to him, and the most important thing was and still is that I'm presentable—then he's proud of me and gives me his affection. He's never made me feel as if I might be worthy of being loved for other reasons. While I know that his clumsy attempts to cheer me up are well intentioned, his words only deepen my misery.

Looking back on our unhappy meeting at the hotel, I'm disturbed by the fact that my father seemed to be having some trouble speaking: He was hard to follow at times, slurring certain words in a way that made it hard to distinguish one word from the next. He spoke like someone who had recently suffered a mild stroke. Could he be hiding news about his health from me? This would be typical of him, as someone who constantly denies his own mortality and likes to joke that he's been gifted with eternal life. In reality, my father's health has been visibly declining for years, and yet he continues to work day and night to save the last remnants of his dying empire. As an economic consultant, he bought a chocolate factory in East Germany after reunification that went bust, which is why he's now heavily in debt and persecuted by his creditors. But since he's ashamed about his wealth disappearing, he hardly mentions this drama. I decide to talk to him about the changes in his speech at the next opportunity.

The mental constitutions of our parents increasingly haunt us as we get older. It's probably even worse when they're dead—then they positively crawl their way into you. While I long sought to distance myself from my father's pessimism, I now realize that it's slowly but surely catching up with me. He used to be entirely dismissive when I told him of the bold new plans I was forging, like my idea to found my own contemporary art journal. "That'll never work" was his credo—his own life had likely offered him little cause for optimism, and so he became one of life's worriers. My mother is the absolute opposite, brimming over with energy and optimism and remaining hopeful in even the direst situations. This can also tip over into toxic optimism at times, when she simply ignores problems instead of dealing with them; her happy nature seems forced and artificial when she downplays other people's pain as she does her own.

    Like my mother, I spent years going through life with boundless optimism, making bold or even outright risky decisions while convinced deep down that everything would somehow always magically work out for the best. I no longer believe in this "lucky child" plot, however, and some things have certainly turned out differently than I had hoped: My books never became bestsellers, for one thing, and I'm not living happily with my partner and children. My father's pessimistic attitude is strengthening its grip on me, and I now habitually expect the worst. I feel rigid with fear when I think of my modest pension, or of how little time I have left to change course in my relationships or finances. At the same time, I battle my pessimistic impulses—my mother's optimism, shining through. I spur myself on, forcing myself to think more positively and reminding myself of how much I've already achieved. But then I hear the whispered voice of my father, telling me that even if I have achieved a lot, it doesn't mean it'll stay that way in the future. And with this, his pessimistic attitude has me back under its grip.

    As a young woman, I thought my parents wouldn't influence me later in life at all, as many in my circle did; the most important thing to me was that I didn't end up like them. Having grown older, however, I have to admit that I'm becoming increasingly like them, physically as well as mentally. I recognize my father in me when I'm photographed now—I show my teeth when I smile like he does, and my eyes are getting ever smaller, like his own. Like my father, I lie in bed awake at night turning over problems in my mind, deprived of sleep by my own worries and anxieties. And if I put on a one-woman show at a dinner by delivering long-winded monologues to the other guests, I reproduce the social behavior of my mother, who always irritated me so much. Both of them—my father and my mother—have shaped my worldview and thinking at the deepest level, and I feel their influence in every decision I make.

My cousin Christopher just called, which rarely happens. While he also lives in Berlin, our different lifestyles mean we have little to do with each other: He works for the city and plays a lot of sports in his free time, whereas I'm usually either sitting at my desk or fulfilling some social obligation in the art scene. While I used to feel sorry for him for what I saw as his less-than-glamorous life, I now envy him not just for his secure government job but above all for the small apartment he owns in Pankow, a leafy district of Berlin. How I wish I'd had his foresight fifteen years ago, when he took out a loan to buy a home that's now worth four times what he paid for it. But I was occupied by other things back then—property didn't interest me. He's now largely paid off the loan and, unlike me, has the security of knowing he can stay in his home as long as he wants to. At least in theory. During our telephone call, he confronts me with the reality: Owning your own property can also be hell. Christopher tells me he can no longer work from home, since his apartment is far too cold. At the last owners' meeting, a majority voted to lower the heating level so much that the radiators can no longer be turned all the way up—an attempt to keep the rapidly rising heating costs under control. As a result, it's now impossible to get his apartment warm in the winter. The building's other residents are also freezing and swap stories of their misery in the stairwell. This situation is made worse by the fact that a "majority owner" pushed through the construction of some small new balconies, which no one actually needs since they face north and are also cold. And so not only is Christopher freezing in his apartment, but he also has to put up with extremely noisy construction work that he claims will last for months. After expressing my sympathy, I offer to let him set up his workspace in my living room; it's warm here, at least, and for all the noise, there's no construction site to deal with.

My conversation with Christopher helps me realize the biggest problem we're currently facing: While the crisis affects us all—theoretically *connecting* us to others—we each see ourselves as lone warriors who must cope with the misery alone. In times of high inflation, it naturally makes a difference whether you have to count every cent or are wealthy enough that increased prices don't affect you. And yet I've observed an attitude of "every man for himself" among my friends, regardless of their class backgrounds. We each work to find a way out for ourselves, losing sight of what connects us to others, which is structural. While we might come from different classes, we're all ultimately subject to the abstract dominance of capitalism, which also affects us mentally. To think we can rise above others and pull ourselves out of the crisis by our own efforts is thus an illusion. I think the current widespread focus on people's individual situations is also the result of decades of social individualization and isolation: Experience being left to deal with your problems and anxieties alone often enough, and you eventually convince yourself that you can only rely on yourself. It's the same with me: Should I ever end up in serious financial trouble, I wouldn't expect anyone to step in and help me. And since I feel out on a limb, I fail to recognize that others—such as Christopher—are experiencing something very similar to myself. Like me, he's ultimately suffering from the current situation, and like me, he's powerless in the face of the majority owner and his machinations. But like everyone else, we hold on to the illusion that there might be a way out for us—a way out that, in reality, doesn't exist for anyone.

I ask myself why I and many of my friends are currently finding it so hard to connect with others, as panic drives each of us to concentrate solely on our own advancement. I turn to Freud, who has much to say about the collective psyche. In *Group Psychology and the Analysis of the Ego*, he describes the phenomenon of the individual whose "panic fear" makes them focus purely on their own welfare as stemming from their recognition that "the emotional ties, which have hitherto made the danger seem small [...] have ceased to exist." When the individual no longer feels emotionally cared for in their collective, then, their panic makes them seek refuge alone and outside of it. The "libidinous structure" of the group is of central importance for Freud: As soon as our collective stops providing us with libidinal satisfaction, our fears begin to grow. According to Freud, the "panic fear" of the individual "presupposes a relaxation in the libidinal structure of the group": Where shared convictions and projects once formed the cement that held our community together, we eventually find ourselves confronted with a splintered social group whose libidinal cohesion is equally fractured. Faced with such a situation, our fear generally drives us to focus exclusively on cultivating our own garden.

It seems to me like this loss of group identity is also reducing our empathy for one another. At the same time, the fact that we do now treat each other with less empathy is partly due to the fact that we don't let others know how we're really feeling. Following the American model, it's become common practice in recent years to show only your brightest and cheeriest side during meetings and social events, and I myself now often put on such an act for my friends and colleagues. In doing so, I signal to them that I'm firmly in control of my life and full of optimism, while in reality I'm plagued by heartbreak, money worries, and sleepless nights. And yet it's also sensible to hide my true feelings from all but my closest friends: I don't want to bother the world with my authentic feelings, for one thing, and for another it's advisable only to show weakness to those you feel emotionally secure with. That I don't reveal my crises to all is thus purely a matter of self-protection. This reticence also has its downsides, however, since by refusing to share my problems, I bottle them up, leaving me to deal with my afflictions alone. And since others don't open up to me either, my encounters with them leave me feeling abandoned and forced to fend for myself. I'll also never know how they're really feeling inside. This game of pretending to have the "perfect life" is currently particularly prevalent in the commercial art world, where you might think everyone is mentally stable and has access to unlimited resources. No one here shows their wounds, as Joseph Beuys once programmatically demanded they do (even if this guarded and patriarchal man never took his own advice).

Speaking of wounds, I'm still not coping well with Antoine's absence. I often imagine him spontaneously flying to Berlin to win me back: I see him approaching me on Kastanienallee, then I run up to him and fall into his arms. All is right again. But the sad truth is that he returned the things I'd left at his apartment by post a few days ago. I opened the package with trembling hands yesterday, hoping to find a peace offering from him. But all I saw was my Mont Blanc ballpoint, some crumpled lingerie, a beach towel, and a few books. Antoine clearly threw these things into the box without any care, as if trying to get rid of them as quickly as possible—making space in his cupboards for his new relationship. It's so humiliating to be passed off and disposed of in this way. I now repeatedly wake up in the middle of the night with pains in my lower abdomen—the mere thought of his new relationship is enough to make me groan. While I try to avoid imagining Antoine in bed with Natalie, images of them having sex constantly force their way into my mind. I often find myself longing for my own destruction, imagining the aforementioned sword piercing through my body and freeing my spirit from its torment. I feel like a wounded animal, hoping someone will save it from its own destructive behavior.

The whole of New York now seems as if it were under a curse—I can't imagine visiting again when I might cross paths with Antoine and Natalie, and with the memory of what I've lost lurking around every corner. I wouldn't survive it. This emotional chaos has reduced my appetite to next to nothing, and I'm becoming ever thinner as a result—the slices of cake I eat each day to cheer myself up don't seem to be making any difference. The only thing that does help is yoga, even if I have to drag myself to my classes. Picking myself up and leaving the house now takes an exceptional amount of discipline. Having done so, however, it always feels as if I've managed to outsmart myself: My mind is still at rock bottom, but my body feels better. At the very least, this gives me hope that I will eventually get over the pain.

On the recommendation of a friend, I booked an appointment with a therapist who has a consultation room in a nice practice on Fasanenplatz in Schöneberg. A black-and-white portrait of Freud hangs over the therapy couch, which naturally appeals to me as a Freud enthusiast. The therapist's name is Frau Dölling. She peers at me sternly through her glasses, and while her fixed gaze and earnest expression are intimidating, they also prevent me from launching into a monologue or putting on a show for her. I dejectedly tell her of my poor psychological state, of my sleeplessness, and of the nightly torments that the mere thought of Antoine's new relationship triggers in me. Frau Dölling dryly remarks that this period of acute pain will soon be over, and that we'll then work together to find out why I entered into a relationship with a man who wasn't prepared to do anything for me and replaced me at the first opportunity. While her comments make me gulp, I also feel seen and supported. At the end of the session, I ask her if we might be able to talk on the phone for the next few weeks, since I'm planning to go on holiday. Her gaze becomes even sterner, and she replies that while she does offer telephone appointments in exceptional circumstances, it's essential at this early stage of our work together that we see each other regularly—at least twice a week, ideally three times. I ask myself if I'm ready to take on such a commitment. Then again, do I have any choice? Since I'm now firmly resolved to break out of my unhealthy pattern of dysfunctional relationships, I see no alternative to therapy. At the same time, I don't want to put my relationship with Frau Dölling above all my other plans—I still want to have my stay by the ocean, where I can recover from my recent emotional ordeal. I tell her I'll think about how often we should meet, and we arrange a session for the following week.

    I'd originally planned to pay for these sessions myself; as a freelancer, I'm privately insured, and if my insurance provider finds out I have psychological problems, they might categorize me as "mentally ill" and massively raise my premiums. I also see my therapy sessions as a private matter. An hour with Frau Dölling costs a hundred euros, however, and I currently don't know how I would find the money for regular sessions. It looks like I'll have to file a claim for reimbursement from my insurer after all. Thinking of my ongoing and constantly rising living costs causes the feelings of anxiety that are constantly lurking within me to instantly rise to the surface. The subject of money has become charged with anxiety for me, and I'm no longer able to feel relaxed about it. Even the idea of keeping a record of my expenses fills me with dread; I don't want to know exactly what I'm spending, which would only put more strain on me. I also find it hard to remember the exact amounts I pay for my living costs each month. I'm often asked how much my rent is, and the number simply refuses to come—I suppress these facts to keep my anxiety under control.

While Ken Honda's bestselling book *Happy Money* advocates living in harmony with our finances, I'm a long way off from this myself. That I see money as something to be feared is demonstrated by the fact that I never look too closely at the contents of my wallet. I refuse to keep track of how much cash I have with me, blindly spending it until there's none left and I have to visit the ATM; should I pay the check in a restaurant, for example, I usually don't even register the amount—a pure defense mechanism. Despite this, I don't correspond to any of the personality types Honda identifies in his book: I'm not neurotically frugal nor do I throw my money out the window. And while money is not unimportant to me, it's also not something I madly chase after. While I would never deny the importance of money in living a fulfilled life, I would never declare it to be the solution to all of life's problems either. My relationship with it is twisted in its own way: I'm entirely capable of acting shrewdly at times in my business dealings—such as when negotiating fees, for example—but I don't know how much money I actually have in my account.

On the subject of fees, it occurs to me that I still have to give a well-paid talk in Karlsruhe before traveling to Gran Canaria next week; thankfully, it's already written. After quickly booking my train ticket, I arrange to meet my mother, who lives near Karlsruhe with her partner. She wants to come to my talk, and to the dinner afterward. We've spoken often on the phone since my dramatic separation from Antoine. I make no attempt to hide my despair from her, in part because she's a specialist in matters of heartbreak: She had countless unhappy affairs after separating from my father, and I still remember how she would spend days on end traipsing around in her dressing gown, constantly in tears. The pain I currently feel from my separation from Antoine could be seen as a continuation of the unhappiness that her own romantic dramas once caused her. I learned from her that men will inevitably only plunge you into emotional misery, and that there's no happiness to be found in relationships. And now, she frequently complains about her current partner's behavior.

Since she's experienced what I'm going through herself, she has more understanding for me than others do. She calls me more regularly now and often offers me good advice, like taking a long hot shower before bed. This relaxes the body and increases the chances of getting a good night's sleep, despite my inner turmoil. I'm looking forward to seeing her, even though our relationship has always been complicated. While my mother has always supported me in my professional ambitions, it's not easy for her to see me doing what *she* herself always wanted to do. She wanted to write children's books, but it never came to anything. Instead, she satisfies her urge to write by penning long and eloquent letters to us, her children, among others. When one of us is sick, these letters are full of advice on how to get better—she usually suggests inhaling hot salt water or using calf wraps against fever. If one of us can't sleep, she proposes that we read a novel from the nineteenth century, and for back pain, she likes to draw us a series of exercises to do during the day. Reading these elaborate and entertaining letters is a joy.

I arrive in Karlsruhe to find my mother waiting for me on the station platform. While I'm admiring her new haircut and sunglasses, she anxiously tells me how worryingly thin I've become. We go to a café, and I order a slice of nut gâteau with cream, as if trying to prove to her that I'm not anorexic. My mother has always worried I might develop an eating disorder. As a teenager, I rejected the meals she prepared, preferring to live off toast and Nutella instead. I think most women of my generation had a neurotic relationship with food, but the point of refusing her food was to avoid ending up like her.

    We make our way to the Academy of Fine Arts, where I'm giving my lecture in the auditorium. It does me good to see my mother there, sitting in the front row and sending me supportive signals. While she normally finds fault with any cultural event, her praise for my lecture is unreserved. The rector of the academy takes us out for pizza afterward with a few colleagues, all of whom are male. The mood gets lively. I'm the only woman at the table apart from my mother, and she tells me later that she now understands what I was up against, working in this field: The men at the table were chivalrous, but they were also incredibly dominant and opinionated.

Sitting in the dining car in the train back to Berlin, I make a serious error: I call Antoine and leave him multiple messages, telling him I urgently need to speak to him. After the fifth attempt, he finally picks up. I ask him how things are going with his new girlfriend, and if he might be missing me a little. I'm well aware that I'm demeaning myself, of course—I hate myself for acting this way, but my desire to hear his voice outweighs my sense of self-worth. Antoine pleads with me not to go down this road and tries to end the call as quickly as possible. The situation is painful for him too, he says, and me contacting him only makes it worse. He's obviously doing all he can to banish me from his life (and thoughts); any hope I had of reconciliation is shattered. I resolve to erase Antoine from my memory following this crushing phone call, and so I begin by immediately deleting any photos of him from my phone. Once home, I set to work on his emails and gifts; my first priority is to get rid of the dress, skirt, and bag he got me from Vanessa Bruno, which I take to a secondhand store around the corner from my apartment. When I've eventually succeeded in ridding my apartment of any mementos of him, a sense of relief comes over me. I feel more confident again.

My therapist has written me an email informing me that our next session will no longer take place at her practice on Fasanenplatz, since financial pressures have forced her to give it up and move to new premises on Gustav-Müller-Strasse. I take the U-Bahn to her new practice, which, to my eyes, seems to physically embody my therapist's diminished social status. She has fallen victim to the thing I fear most: being forced to move to a dark and chilly basement flat because of an unaffordable rent rise. The street itself is also less than inviting, strewn with old pieces of furniture that the former owners have "donated" to the local community. Standing in front of my therapist's building, I encounter an elderly lady who seems totally disoriented, talking loudly to herself and searching in vain for her key. I accompany her into the hallway and lead her to the floor where she claims her apartment is; her mental instability seems to have something prophetic about it, as if warning me that this building will drive you mad. I enter my therapist's small, dark, and cold waiting room, which would rob even the most cheerful person of their optimism. I sit there alone, waiting for Frau Dölling to punctually call me into the consultation room for my session. While the portrait of Freud has been rehung here, it does nothing to brighten the gloomy atmosphere. I keep my jacket on to protect myself from the chill rising from the floor, while Frau Dölling herself wears giant fluffy slippers, as if trying to demonstrate how cold it is in here. I don't have the courage to tell her how much her move to these less salubrious premises is affecting me emotionally. Frau Dölling wants us to set the terms of our work together: We're to meet twice a week, and to speak on the phone once a week during my three weeks on Gran Canaria so there's no break in our sessions. She presents me with a sort of therapy contract, in which I commit to staying in Berlin for the next three years. Long absences are unhelpful, she says. And should I become seriously ill, I must inform her forty-eight hours in advance, or I'll still be charged for the sessions I miss. So, Frau Dölling is demanding that I enter into a binding relationship with her. This therapy is starting to feel more like a corset. I presume the purpose of this exercise is to teach me to take responsibility and not run away. While I give in and sign the contract in my desperation, I already know I'll cancel some appointments at the last minute. I can feel resentment rising within me; by issuing this travel ban, Frau Dölling is taking away my freedom of movement. There'll be no more spontaneous trips away in the future. Instead, I'll have to stay here and work on myself—not a pleasant prospect.

Having arrived back home, I start packing for my trip to Gran Canaria. My friend advised me to be prepared for all kinds of weather, so I load up my suitcase with both summer and winter clothes. It's far too heavy, of course. I treat myself to a taxi to the airport—it's beyond the budget I set for myself for the holiday, but I don't have the strength to drag this monstrous suitcase around behind me. From the second I set off, I feel exposed and unstable. My last trip away was to visit Antoine, which promised me security; now I'm traveling to put him behind me, and it feels wrong and full of risk. Gerald stands waiting for me at the check-in desk. Seeing him standing there, it suddenly dawns on me that I'll be living in the house of a man I barely know. I'm already developing slight aversions to him, simply because he's not Antoine; even the fact that he uses a different aftershave than my ex makes me aggressive. How will I ever survive three weeks living with this man, who does nothing for me physically at all?

We land on Gran Canaria. Gerald has rented us a car and drives us to the house. He drives far worse than Antoine does, unfortunately, abruptly braking and clumsily changing gears. When we arrive, I discover a pool, which significantly improves my mood. Gerald shows me my room, which has an en suite bathroom and sits in a side building—so we'll only bump into each other in the kitchen and on the terrace. I quickly unpack, and we drive to the beach. The sun beams down on us, and I notice how the mere sight of the ocean makes me feel better. Stretched out on the beach, my body relaxes, and I feel a growing sense of happiness. But this tender bliss evaporates the moment I see someone surfing: Antoine is also a keen surfer. I discuss with Gerald whether one of these well-built surfers might serve as a sort of "transitional object," a temporary lover to take the place of Antoine until the worst of the heartbreak is behind me. Gerald tells me of his own separation from a young dancer who secretly slept with other men while pretending that he was the only one who really mattered. This drama dragged on for months, and the fact that she ended it deeply affected him. Here we are on Gran Canaria, then, two emotional casualties hoping to recover with the help of the sun, sea, and sand.

Unfortunately, the nights here are also terrible—almost worse than at home, in fact. I'm protected by the familiar in my bedroom back in Berlin, where I can stave off the worst anxiety attacks with a hot-water bottle or a cup of tea. Lying here in this unfamiliar room, I'm exposed to all my fears and worries and entirely at their mercy. It's the same feeling I get in hotel rooms, where I can never fall asleep—as if all the worries of the world have collapsed upon me. Lacan writes somewhere that Freud's theory that anxiety is an objectless fear is wrong; according to him, this fear doesn't really occur without an object but is instead a "subjective translation" of what he calls "object *a*." But where is this "object *a*," which we subjects experience as fear, located? According to Lacan, it is found where we speak of ourselves, in the unconscious part of this "I." We thus carry our anxieties around with us but are unable to escape them, since they essentially make us who we are. I know this only too well. It makes no difference whether I try to distract myself with other thoughts or with a book—I'm always thrown back onto myself and my anxiety-ridden unconscious. I find it hard to give a more precise definition of this fear. It's not the fear of being abandoned; I already have been. It's more a fear of what I am, of what is, and of what will be. I'm plagued by memories of what I've lost, or of arguments with Antoine. At the same time, I imagine a lonely future in which I never meet anyone else. I wake up with a start during the night, missing Antoine's body next to me. I feel a strong urge to call him, but giving in to it only makes me despise myself. Thankfully, I only reach his voicemail this time.

Gerald and I meet on the sun-filled terrace for breakfast. He says the house belongs to his uncle, who lets him use it now and then free of charge. We discuss our respective attitudes to money. Gerald works as a journalist and tells me that money means nothing at all to him. He grew up in the DDR, where it didn't matter, and while it's important to him in symbolic terms that his work is recognized, the monetary aspect simply doesn't interest him. I ask him if the current decline in print media isn't making him fear for his own existence. He tells me that this doesn't worry him, since he has a plan B: He's a licensed taxi driver, and so he always has something to fall back on if his career as a journalist ever comes to an end. Luxury and status symbols don't matter to him anyway; the only things he does care about are eating well and regularly spending time in nature. I find this astonishing. If only my own aspirations were so modest.

    Gerald tells me he plans to use his time at the house to work on a book about the current crisis in journalism. We agree to each work in our rooms in the mornings and travel to the beach together in the afternoons; in the evenings, we'll either cook something at home or go to a casual restaurant. He tells me he had trouble sleeping last night. Stress always catches up with him at the beginning of a holiday, he says; his thoughts start spinning like crazy, as if the more peaceful lifestyle were giving his stress the space it needs to unfold. When I tell him about my own nocturnal anxieties, he's clearly taken aback that I'm tormented in this way. He tells me he's always seen me as a relatively fearless person—as a sort of alpha woman who forges ahead with her career plans without letting the reactions of others throw her off track. He even admits that my single-mindedness made him a little scared of me. I'm astounded by this—do I really come across as frightening or intimidating to others? Or is this just a projection—the defensive reaction of a man who feels threatened and "castrated" by a woman's ambition? I'm probably being too easy on myself by attributing Gerald's anxiety to his gender, however—a close female friend also recently confided to me that she has always been slightly intimidated by my enormous workload, seeming self-confidence, and professional ambition. She told me she sometimes finds my manner to be monstrously dominant, above all when I'm standing at a podium delivering a monologue. The thought that both she and Gerald see me this way leaves me speechless. It never occurred to me that others might find me intimidating; I'm too preoccupied with my *own* anxieties and their causes, whether internal or external. Would they find my behavior as intimidating if I were a man, I wonder? Since I can't experience myself from the outside, I'm unable to judge whether their view of me is justified or not. In any case, I'll try to be more aware of how I conduct myself during lectures in the future, and to develop a better sense of how the audience is reacting.

    I ponder the question of how much it's even possible to influence the feelings of others. Can I really change their perception of me, so that they no longer see me as threatening or overbearing? Or are their reactions beyond my control? I could be more open about my anxieties, of course—baring my misery on the social stage for all to see would be a tacit admission of my own shortcomings. And yet this would most likely be interpreted as the hyperconfident gesture of a self-assured woman, which would make me seem even more intimidating. I quickly realize that it's an illusion to think we can control the reactions of others—how they perceive me and what they project onto me is ultimately up to them.

My mother just called and told me about her dog, who pulled so hard on the leash during their walk today that she was barely able to keep hold of him; the second he sees children, he pounces on them. While this dog is dangerous and badly behaved, she says she feels safer with him by her side. I did my best to convince her to give him away, arguing that he could end up pulling her off her feet and injuring a child. But she's determined to keep him at any cost and broke off the conversation. Her stubborn insistence on keeping this unpredictable dog reminds me how she often refused to let go of other toxic love interests. Even though my father had a new, quite unsympathetic wife, she remained close to him and even went on holidays with them. Could it be that I've inherited her predilection for unhealthy attachments?

For all my mother's boundless optimism, I wonder if she might have also passed on some of her anxieties to me. She had a horrific experience shortly after separating from my father in which she was raped by an intruder in her bedroom one night. She would always sleep with the window open, and since our apartment was at ground level, all her rapist had to do was climb into her room; he'd been targeting single women in the area and had already attacked many others, as the police later told us. I must have been around fifteen when this happened. My mother gave no clue of what she had been through, maintaining her composure, hiding her fear, and seemingly refusing to let the whole experience shake her. As she told us time and again, the most important thing to her was that nothing had happened to her daughters.

From that point on, I was afraid of men. I would cycle home at night with my heart pounding, imagining a rapist in every bush waiting to pull me off my bicycle. Public spaces became places of constant fear for me: I would only sit next to older women in the S-Bahn, and I avoided busy carriages in the U-Bahn in case I would be pestered, instead preferring to wait until the next train. If I took a taxi home after going out at night, I would often ask the driver to wait until I was inside before leaving; if I walked home, I always kept my key in my hand so I could quickly stick it in the lock if needed. When cell phones arrived, it was a common trick among young women to make phone calls (or pretend to) when walking alone at night to prevent anyone from harassing them. Hearing steps behind me would make me turn around in alarm or cross the street, and I did my best to avoid large groups of men. Many women of my generation display similar behaviors, and I think that feeling so anxious in public spaces and being constantly on your guard must leave its mark on you. It would never occur to me to visit a bar alone at night, for example;

I only do such things with friends. I also don't like traveling alone.

Gerald and I sit together for dinner in a restaurant by the ocean, already slightly tanned and enjoying the good life. From the corner of my eye, I see that my mother is calling. Since we usually only ever speak to each other in the morning, I feel a sense of foreboding rising in me that something terrible might have happened. My worst fears are confirmed the moment she speaks: "Something has happened to your father," she tells me. He suffered a stroke while working in the garden and is now in a stroke unit in Hamburg. The right side of his body is paralyzed, and he can neither speak nor swallow. Stunned by this news, I ask my mother if I should come immediately. She does her best to keep me away: He's in good hands, she says, and there's nothing I can do for him there at the moment. If I want more details, I can ask Susanna, his wife, who found him in the garden. I ask my mother how long he had been lying there, but she doesn't know. She tells me to try to stay calm, and to continue with my holiday and visit my father when I return. I feel as if I'm lost in a fog, unable to grasp what's happening. I despair at the thought that my father, who always chose his words so carefully, has now lost the ability to speak altogether; the idea of him lying helpless and speechless in a hospital bed fills me with an overwhelming and crushing sense of pity. Gerald tries to reassure me; he knows of many stroke patients who went on to make full recoveries, he says. But I know instinctively that this stroke is a death sentence for my father. Without the ability to speak or swallow, he'll never survive. I reluctantly call my stepmother. I begin by asking her how serious the stroke was; she replies that it was "moderately serious," but I can tell from the tone of her voice that she's not telling the truth. There's no doubt in my mind that he suffered a *severe* stroke that damaged his language center and paralyzed his muscles. Like my mother, Susanna tries to stop me from immediately boarding a plane: I'm not needed at the moment and should come after my holiday, she says, when he's had some time to recover. But an inner voice tells me I should be by my father's side right now, and to pack my things and leave immediately.

Following a sleepless night, I keep my telephone appointment with Frau Dölling the following morning. I tell her about my father's stroke and the despair I'm feeling, which brings us to the subject of emotional loneliness. I tell her how getting through his illness without the emotional support of a partner would take strength I don't have. And how I long for someone who will care for and support me in this situation. We talk about why Antoine wasn't this person and couldn't have been. I recall a situation one Christmas when Antoine was visiting me in Berlin— briefly, as always—and my father's life seemed to be in danger. My father was on holiday in Turkey with Susanna when news reached me of a devastating earthquake in the region they were in; my sister and I didn't know where they were staying, so we called around all the five-star hotels looking for them. At some point we found him—he and his wife were both fine. In the anxious hours before we knew what had happened to my father, Antoine informed me that he unfortunately had to cut his trip short and leave the next morning, since he had to attend an important business meeting in New York. If something had happened to my father back then, I would have been forced to deal with the situation alone, as I am now. Antoine had other priorities and wasn't there for me. Now my father's preparing to leave this world, and I have no partner by my side—while I still have my siblings, my mother, and my friends, they are unable to compensate for this deficit.

    I call my old friend Gisela from Hamburg. After explaining my father's situation to her, she kindly offers to accompany me to the hospital for my first visit. I'm deeply touched by this gesture, and I try to practice gratitude for her support. I find it incredibly difficult to celebrate the positive events in my life, however. I often barely even register them, fixating on the negative aspects of life instead of seeing how much support I do actually receive from others, in spite of everything. Even when I do experience something positive, it's filtered through my perception of my wider circumstances, as if they were surrounded by a cloud of negativity that doesn't let anything good through. Then again, it's not reasonable to expect myself to focus on the positives in my life when my father is so ill. The shock I feel at his condition overrides everything else. I book a flight back to Germany for tomorrow, and I'm glad I'll soon be there, where I can see how he's doing for myself.

I've been thinking a lot about my father lately. He has always symbolized prosperity in my life, and for a long time, I could rely on his financial support. It was thanks to him that I was able to study in France, for which I'm enormously grateful. My delusional image of myself as a rich kid is also due to this support, since my confident manner is in no small part a result of his wealth. I spent a long time feeling financially secure, as if nothing could happen to me. And this often was the case: If I was unable to pay an electricity bill at the end of the month, for example, my father paid it for me. Paradoxically, I continued to feel I had this safety net even after he had gone broke; his massive debts at the bank did nothing to change the fact that he was the money man in my life. Even when he was no longer able to continue paying for his private health insurance, I didn't wake up from this dream, unconsciously continuing to assume that he would support me if I ever ended up in trouble. I wasn't ready to relieve him of his role. At the same time, everything had changed. There had once been a time when he would often slip me banknotes or buy me an expensive dress, but this all stopped at some point. When a mistake by my tax adviser forced me to make a large back payment, my father was unable to give me any money, and I had to borrow it from another relative. My father still lives well—in a house with a garden, with an S-Class out front and expensive holidays. But the well has run dry for us children. It doesn't matter; I've gotten enough from him already. But I'm left wondering whether he's getting proper treatment now that he's no longer privately insured. Or are they only doing the minimum for him?

I'm sitting in the waiting area at Gran Canaria airport, about to take my flight back to Hamburg. Gerald dropped me off—he's staying on alone. I'm secretly relieved that I won't have to spend the next few weeks negotiating shared holiday plans with this man, whose mere presence is now enough to put me on edge. There's nothing he can do about this, of course; it isn't his fault I'm constantly wishing Antoine were here in his place.

I try to picture my imminent visit to my father's hospital bed. It isn't easy—the idea that he's no longer able to communicate is simply too horrible to accept.

I prepare myself by reading Didier Eribon's new book on my Kindle, about his elderly mother who was sent to a care home against her will. When she moves in, he witnesses a conversation between her and an old acquaintance in which they talk about their late ex-husbands— how dreadful these men were, and how they made their lives hell. Eribon realizes that his mother—like so many women of her generation—was never really entirely happy in her marriage. She came from a working-class background and worked as a cleaner her entire life. Her problems were in no way comparable with my own. And yet for all our differences, we were each largely unhappy in our relationships. Women of all social backgrounds know how dispiriting life with a man can be; for many, their fear of being alone or of financial repercussions makes them stay with men who they basically despise. Like Eribon's mother and her friend, they swap stories about these men and their unreasonable behavior. I can imagine these women finding a new lease on life after their husbands die, enjoying their newfound freedom just as

Eribon describes his mother doing. His mother's freedoms were always short-lived, however. She was plagued by the ailments of old age just a few years after her husband's death, and any freedom she did have was gone by the time she moved into the care home. Thinking of her fate and those of my unhappily married friends and acquaintances makes me promise myself that I will never again subject myself to the torture of an unhappy relationship. Then again, isn't it presumptuous of me to insist on my own happiness? Doesn't life teach us instead that making compromises and accepting the shortcomings of others is essential, particularly in relationships? My therapist often speaks of the need to tolerate ambivalences in romantic relationships, and Freud repeatedly points out that love and hate are close to one another. But how are we to know when the negative feelings that are a natural part of any relationship have tipped over into unnecessary and agonizing suffering because of one's partner? On the one hand, we're repeatedly told that relationships require effort, and that there's no such thing as the "perfect man"; on the other, we have to be capable of recognizing when enough is enough. Is it time to leave when all we feel toward the other person is resentment and resignation? Or should we do our best to "put up" with them, and to tolerate these ambiguities? Boarding begins.

I'm sitting in the taxi on the way from Hamburg Airport to the hospital in Altona, my stomach cramped with tension; the closer we get to our destination, the worse it becomes. Waiting for me at the entrance is Gisela, who immediately takes me in her arms. Unfortunately, we bump into Susanna in the elevator, fresh from visiting my father. Her garishly colorful and wildly patterned outfit seems entirely out of place in these depressing surroundings. She immediately starts barking questions at me: Why did I come when she told me I wasn't needed here right now? Shooting a glance at my friend, she adds that there's no way I can bring her with me when I visit him; he doesn't want any visitors while he's in this condition, family excepted. I ask myself how she can be so sure of this when he's unable to speak. We quickly walk away, leaving my ranting stepmother behind us. My nose is filled with the distinctive smell of hospital disinfectant, which used to make me feel sick as a child and still does. I'm scared to see my father in his current state, and I barely register my surroundings in my agitation.

I open the door to his room as if I were in a trance. My father is sitting upright in bed with his eyes wide open. His mouth is crooked, and he's extremely emaciated. I barely recognize him. He sees me and starts wildly gesticulating with his working arm, making guttural noises—he obviously wants to tell me something. It's frightening. I can tell by his expression that something is upsetting him. He looks furious. The nurse who joins us to administer his medication explains to me that stroke victims suffer from extreme mood swings and emotional instability. Their behavior resembles that of young children, she says, where outbursts of extreme rage can quickly give way to moments of great tenderness. I try to calm my father down. His fingernails and toenails are extremely long, which makes him look neglected—clearly no one bothered to take care of them. I happen to have my mini travel manicure set with me and decide to file his nails, which he seems to enjoy. It's impossible to communicate with him, however—even simple questions that could be answered with a mere nod or shake of the head are beyond his understanding. He repeatedly flings his arm toward me in his rage. Seeing that he wants to tell me something but is unable to breaks my heart. He's being fed through a gastric tube, since the muscles used for swallowing have been paralyzed. Saliva drips down constantly onto his filthy T-shirt. I look in the cupboard for something clean to put on him, but there's nothing in there. When I call Susanna and ask her to bring him some clean shirts, she brusquely replies that he doesn't have any, and that I should buy some for him. I realize that she's deliberately neglecting him—even worse, that she's taking revenge on him for all he's done to her. He never treated her well, always looking down on her, and now she's paying him back for it. In my memory, they were an awful couple who only ever communicated with one another in irritated, spiteful tones. Their relationship was not based on love but a financial deal. He met her in Hungary, not long before the Wall came down; twenty-five years younger than him, she got together with this freshly divorced West German man with three kids in the hope of living a life of luxury. He couldn't be alone and needed a quick replacement for my mother. A disaster foretold.

    Gisela and I visit a local shopping center, where I buy a pack of T-shirts in my father's size. It feels good to be doing something for him, so I buy him a bottle of aftershave to cover up the horrible smell of the hospital ward. I also buy a small television, to give him something else to focus on. Then again, will he even be able to use it? Back in his room, I speak with his doctor, who tells me that my father is no longer "legally competent"; Susanna has power of attorney and will make all decisions relating to him from now on. I realize I've been totally stripped of any power as his daughter—Susanna can let my father lie around rotting in a filthy T-shirt, and all I can do is watch.

Gisela and I drive to a café situated on the banks of the Elbe near the hospital. Since my childhood, the area along the river has been transformed into a sort of lifestyle zone, with people in swimsuits now relaxing with drinks where we once took long and bracing walks, our rubber boots and raincoats shielding us against the stiff breeze. Some even swim in the river, which must have undergone some sort of cleaning process in the meantime; the brackish water and raw sea air are long gone, just as my father's earlier personality was erased by his stroke. Gisela and I discuss the situation. While I consider taking my father back to Berlin with me and caring for him there, he could hardly stay at my apartment while he's being fed artificially. Nor would Susanna ever agree to such a situation in the first place. I call several local speech therapists who were recommended to me by the hospital: My greatest hope is that my father will learn to speak and swallow again with their help. I eventually reach a friendly therapist who agrees to work with my father on a private basis. The relief I feel at this instantly brightens my mood—I feel less dejected. But I also realize that I'm unable to spend the coming night in either my father's house or my former home with my mother. I'm not welcome at my father's, and visiting the small terraced house I once shared with my mother and siblings instantly plunges me back into the depression of a child forced to adjust to more modest conditions after her parents have separated. I never got used to my bedroom at my mother's house, which isn't decorated to my taste—the walls are painted in a hideous shade of lime green, and the sight of the horrible linoleum floor still bothers me to this day. A lot of the space is taken up by a garish, bulky wardrobe that once housed my things alongside my mother's. That room always felt alien to me. Returning to it isn't an option, even in the greatest emergency. I decide to book a hotel room for the night so I can visit my father again the next day. While I've been distancing myself from my biological family and trying to reinvent myself for years now, the misery of my childhood in Hamburg always catches up with me. Eribon provides a fitting description of this mechanism in his book about his mother, arguing that familial parameters continue to shape us even when we believe we've long put them behind us. For Eribon, however, it's the *social* status of our family alone that leaves its mark on us. I would challenge him on this point. For while there's no doubt that my parents' class backgrounds played an important role in forging my own self-image, I see the *psychological* constitution formed during childhood as even more influential. The anguish of the abandoned child who never feels at home has been with me throughout my entire life.

    Now slightly panicked, I phone around a few hotels in the area—they're all fully booked. No amount of money could get me to sleep in my old bed at my mother's house, where I'd only slip back into my old, familiar misery. Hotel rooms might not offer any protection against pain and worry, but the fact that I've chosen to be there makes me feel less powerless than I do in her home. I eventually find a vacant room in a "boutique hotel" in Blankenese, a wealthy suburb in the west of the city. Gisela offers to drive me there, and I gratefully accept.

I have to admit something to myself. I sent Antoine a text message yesterday, informing him about my father's stroke; he sent a brief reply, saying he was sorry to hear it. Unfortunately, I didn't leave it at this short exchange but fired off multiple further text messages to him, which went unanswered. It's the first time in my life I've been ghosted, and all I can say is it feels awful. The silence at the other end makes me constantly ask myself what I've done wrong. What is he punishing me for? Could one of my messages have been tactless or overly intrusive? There are numerous forums online where victims of ghosting can discuss their experiences. Those using these forums take the view that it's not the person being ghosted that's the problem, but the person doing the ghosting: Anyone who acts this way is afraid of conflict, narcissistic, and lacking in empathy, they claim, and so they break off contact in this passive-aggressive manner. Even worse, anyone who ghosts another person makes it impossible for them to find closure. I can't believe how brutally Antoine is acting toward me. Am I not going through an acute crisis that makes our problems seem insignificant in comparison? And isn't it a human imperative to show care to someone in this situation? Or am I not worthy of such treatment in his eyes? Why is he avoiding me? Could it be that he wants to spare me the pain of hearing him mention his new girlfriend, or is it because he simply can't be bothered to deal with me? I also hate myself for turning to Antoine, of all people, in my despair. He was never there for me when it mattered, so why should it be any different this time? Then again, he might feel manipulated, as if I'm using the situation with my father to force him to pay attention to me. But why would he teach me this lesson now, at a time when I'm losing my father? Can't he put it off until I'm more emotionally stable? I know from the two blue ticks on my WhatsApp messages to him that he's read them. He's just choosing to leave them on read. The fact that he's even capable of acting this way speaks volumes about his character—by ghosting me, he's showed me who he really is. He might even be doing me a favor, since by acting so coldly he's *forcing* me to abandon hope, and to finally realize that he was not the right man for me. And yet the disappointment I feel at his behavior only adds to my burden. I'm so thankful to have my friend Gisela here—someone I can share my pain with, and who actually understands me. We drink a cup of tea together after we've arrived at the hotel, then my retreat to my hotel room can't be delayed any longer. I've forgotten my melatonin tablets and am prepared for the worst. The mattress is soft, and all I have to keep me warm is a thin quilt, leaving me freezing and restless. Fear really does eat the soul. An anxious vision appears to me. I imagine Antoine going around New York and complaining to others about me—how I won't leave him in peace, bombarding him with text messages and invading his privacy. And he would be right. Now fully convinced he's badmouthing me, I lie in bed worrying how this will affect my professional reputation. No one will invite me to conferences anymore, since I'll be seen as a pitiful woman who has no control over her emotions and humiliates herself. My image as a self-assured thinker is going down the drain. There's nothing I can do about it from Hamburg, however; all I can do is try to make sure I don't commit any similar violations in the future.

    The more caught up I get in these thoughts, the more hopeless my chances of sleep become. Now wide awake, I reach for my Kindle and open a book by Karl Ove Knausgård, whose long-winded writing style always has a soporific effect on me. At some point, I drift off into an uneasy sleep, only to be woken up again by the shocking image of my father, arm raised and eyes wide, wanting to tell me something but unable to do so. I force myself to think of something more pleasant—like an island with a beach and palm trees. But who do I want there with me? There's no one I'd want to explore such a place with at this point in my life; I'm entirely alone. Again, I feel waves of anxiety roll through my body, forcing the sweat from my pores. It's lucky I brought an extra pair of pajamas. Things can't go on like this.

The following day, my sister, Sylvia, joins us at the hospital. Her attempt at making contact with our father is far more successful than my own: She brought her violin with her, and he visibly enjoys it when she plays something for him—he smiles slightly, and we recognize his old laugh from behind his crooked lips. We try to communicate with him nonverbally, but we're unsure whether he actually understands anything at all. The attendant physician, an experienced and professional-seeming doctor named Schönebeck, asks us to attend a "family conference" in an adjoining room, together with Susanna. Dr. Schönebeck informs us that he's unfortunately unable to keep my father in the clinic any longer, first since he's not a private patient, and second because he's a hopeless case. The doctor asks Susanna to start looking for a place for my father in a care home. When I ask him if there's any chance that my father will learn to speak and swallow again, he's skeptical; my father's stroke was a particularly severe one, he says, and the speech therapist's efforts at rehabilitation have been unsuccessful until now. We return to my father's room feeling deflated and sad.

The speech therapist I hired arrived during our conversation with the doctor and is now attempting to make words out of printed letters with my father. She starts by laying out his surname, SCHINEIS, before taking the letter *N* away. My father is supposed to complete it again. He puts down a *U*. Doesn't he even know his own name anymore? Or did he not understand the task? We're horrified by the extent of his loss of mental capacity. My sister asks him simple questions that he's supposed to answer by nodding or shaking his head, but it looks as if he's simply guessing the answers. We're unsure how much he's really aware of what's going on. Does he even recognize us? Does he understand what happened to him? I realize that I've already lost my father, without ever having had the opportunity to say goodbye to him. He's drifted away to another world. Then again, this hard-edged and emotionally distant man is now obviously able to access his own emotions in a way he once couldn't; should Susanna enter the room, for example, his face darkens and he looks downright furious, whereas care from me or my sister is rewarded with a blissful smile. I think his current martyrdom might have a higher meaning—perhaps the point is to help him have some emotional experiences at the end of his life? I take his hand, and he holds onto me tight, not wanting to let go. Perhaps I should try to find accommodation near his care home, so I can spend as much time as possible with him before he leaves us forever.

It's now evening, and I'm sitting alone by my father's hospital bed. He suddenly begins gesticulating violently; it's obvious he has something on his mind. I list the possible reasons for him: Does he want to see one of his nurses, or a pastor? Would he like it if I brought him a bottle of his favorite wine? While he's no longer capable of drinking on his own, I could at least wet his lips with it. He shakes his head wildly. I'm clearly on the wrong track. The subject of my father's will comes into my mind at some point. Does he want us to bring it to him so he can alter something in it? He confirms this by vigorously nodding his head up and down, so I call Susanna and ask her to bring it with her to the hospital. While she's reluctant at first, she eventually gives in when I make it clear that checking his will is likely to be his *final wish*. He wrote it by hand a few years ago, according to her. But I also know that he's unable to change anything in it now, since he's no longer deemed to be legally competent. I feel an anxious sense of foreboding rising in me: Is it possible he disinherited us children and is now realizing it was a mistake? Does he want to remove his unloved wife from the will and put us in her place? He once told me Susanna has the right to remain in the house for the rest of her life if she chooses to—does he now want to bequeath it to us instead? Or is this just wishful thinking on my part, since in reality he's not even able to understand the concept of a will and just happened to nod when I mentioned it? I'm groping in the dark; it's unbearable not to know what it is that's bothering him so much. For him to be unable to express his wishes must be torture too. I decide to use this opportunity to make my peace with him. I begin by thanking him for all the financial support he gave me during my studies. It was thanks to his money that I was able to study in Paris. He bursts into tears, which totally floors me. I've never seen my father cry before. Could the fact that he's now so overcome with emotion be a result of the stroke, or is the knowledge that his life is coming to an end making him softer? I'm now in tears myself, and in between my clumsy attempts at consoling him, I regret thanking him for all he's done for me. At the same time, it's nice, in a way, that we're able to shed tears together in this situation; such intimacy between us would have been totally unthinkable before his stroke. My father has always been one of those men who never loses his composure or shows his emotions. While it scares me to see he no longer has control over himself, it's also a genuine relief. Especially since he has every reason to despair.

It's time to take the train back to Berlin. As always, the crowds of people waiting on the platform indicate my train will be totally packed. Rail travel has become torture since the pandemic, and stations are now crisis zones that I battle my way through, constantly dodging those frantically bustling around me and doing my best to get out as unscathed as possible. This is made even more difficult by the fact that the rules are constantly changing, with many trains leaving from a different platform than the one announced, or canceled altogether. Delays are a given, and the chances the cars will be in the same order as stated on the platform are slim. You have to be prepared for anything and extremely quick to react. It's also advisable to book a seat several weeks in advance, since they inevitably sell out, forcing anyone without a reservation to stand.

    I usually give in to the chaos and immediately head to the dining car, which used to be one of my favorite places. Seats there are now also hotly contested, and the only food available is prepackaged—no fresh scrambled eggs, just a microwaved chili con carne or a bland soup. Since the automatic coffee machines are frequently out of service, they often don't even have hot drinks, and countless cost-saving measures by the operators have left the staff totally overstretched and worn out. Rail travel used to be a meditative experience for me: I'd eat a turkey salad in the dining car and look out the window or read, using the time to come up with new ideas. Now the other passengers yell so loudly into their cell phones that any attempt at concentration fails. Spontaneously boarding a train is also out of the question, since passengers are now required to book a ticket and a seat before getting on. Should you miss your train, you have to buy a new ticket, which isn't possible on the train itself. Boarding without one is considered fare evasion. I've developed a neurotic anxiety around rail travel in light of all these recent developments—it's stressful to be at the mercy of such a dysfunctional system. From the moment I step on the train, for example, I'm unsure whether it will actually reach its destination, and I break into a cold sweat any time it slows down or stops unexpectedly. Is there a casualty on the track, perhaps, or a "signal failure" that means I'll end up arriving hours later than I should? What should I do if I end up stranded somewhere for the night because I missed my connection? I try to adopt a Buddhist attitude in such moments, telling myself that everything serves a higher cause and should be welcomed. I endeavor to abandon myself to the chaos of the German railway system, enjoying the loss of control; should there happen to be a delay, I could happily use the time to read or catch up on my emails, instead of getting worked up about it. And yet my serenity is repeatedly interrupted by the rage I feel at my own powerlessness: I want to break free of these trains.

 I gaze through the window, envying the inhabitants of the cozy country houses dotted along the route. Wouldn't life be better there, without the need for public appearances and the constant pressure to perform and compete? Then again, is there really such a thing as a stress-free life by the railway tracks? Living in the immediate vicinity of a high-speed rail line involves the burden of the accompanying dreadful noise pollution. I'm actually relatively lucky in my apartment in Berlin, which, for all the noise, seems like a peaceful retreat in comparison. This thought fills me with a sense of joy and gratitude for my life. While I feel crushed by the double blow of my father's illness and my separation from Antoine, I also know that I live a relatively privileged life, in spite of everything. As stressful as train journeys are, then, they also have the benefit of taking me out of my everyday reality—having some distance from my situation instantly makes me realize how lucky I am to be in my position.

My relief doesn't last long, however, and cabin fever sets in almost as soon as I've stepped through the door to my apartment. I call one friend after another, but all I reach are their voicemails. The idea that people actually used to answer the phone when it rang seems almost unimaginable today; no one is available to talk on the phone anymore, with each of us barricaded away behind our phones switched to voicemail.

I reflect upon how, ever since childhood, I've fought for the attention of people who don't actually treat me well. It began with my father, who showed me barely any appreciation even when I did perform exceptionally well and did pirouettes for him. The greater my achievements as a child—if I won a writing competition or got particularly good grades, for example—the higher his standards became. For him, my brilliance was simply to be expected—I was *his* daughter, after all. And since I wanted to be seen and loved by him for who I am at any cost, I would do more and more in my efforts to impress him. But he was never really interested in me; all that mattered to him was that I looked good, performed well, and didn't create any problems for him. I still carry the pain of not being seen by him.

As with Antoine, I've often sought out relationships that continued this unhealthy pattern of behavior. Antoine never really got involved with me either—getting to know the real me didn't interest him. And this was precisely why I was so attracted to him: I wanted to prove my value to him, so that he would finally grant me his love and recognition. I always showed my best side when I was with him, diligently dressing myself up and sparkling during social events. But nothing helped: Like my father before him, he, too, took me for granted.

For decades now, I've been maintaining a similarly uneven relationship with an art historian friend of mine. She was clearly above me in the social hierarchy when we met, back in the late 1980s. I still had to prove myself. While the balance of power between us has become more complicated in the time since, this "friend" still ensures I remain in second place in our relationship. My texts are either sharply criticized or totally ignored by her; they're never good enough in her eyes. And while I give her elaborate gifts, even paying for a joint trip to Paris for a special birthday, all I get on such occasions is a paltry text message. And this is precisely why I continue to fight for her favor—I support her in her research, and I recently invited her to participate in a conference I organized. The more I do for her, the worse she treats me. She finally broke off contact with me a few days ago, claiming she was unhappy with the seat allocated to her at the dinner after the conference; in reality, she probably just couldn't stand the fact that the event was successful, and that I'm gaining ground in the academic world. Even the text I wrote on her last book failed to earn me any praise—her only response was to send me a minor correction. Why do I put up with all of this, hanging on to a "friendship" that brings me nothing but pain and humiliation? Because I've never known it to be any other way. Deep down, I'm probably still hoping she'll eventually recognize the quality of my work and my value as a person—that at some point I'll have won her over. Then she'll finally be nice to me and lavish me with attention—or so I hope.

I can hardly bear our relationship hanging in the balance like this, and I feel a strong urge to call her and ask what's actually going on. Thankfully, I don't give in, which would earn me nothing but further insults. I have to finally break out of this role as the one who makes all the effort in this relationship. I've got to cut her out of my life. It's unfortunate that our careers mean our paths are bound to cross repeatedly in the future. While I'd usually do everything I could to get our relationship back to normal, in this case, self-preservation demands I make a clean break from her.

I worry that she'll denigrate me and my work to others after we've separated. All too often, I've witnessed her discrediting others in our circle, with serious consequences for their reputations—for she has influence, and she wields it with downright malice. There's already a rivalry between us in any case, since for years now we've been fighting for dominance in certain social spaces, and for the same friends. In my good moments, I resolve to continue the battle; in bad ones, I feel as if I'd rather just admit defeat and leave the field to her. Unfortunately, my career means I can't afford any such retreat, and so I'll continue to compete for the favor of others, making new relationships and friendships and sticking to my plans. I just won't let her be involved in them in the future.

I'm in the Gemäldegalerie, admiring one of my favorite paintings by Rembrandt: *Moses Breaking the Tablets of the Law*, from 1659. I'm fascinated by the way this painting brings a long-finished process into the present: In creating the painting, Rembrandt smeared the brown paint onto the canvas in a way that not only draws attention to the substance of the paint but also highlights the process of painting itself. On the one hand, this image conceals the actual conditions its creator was working under, as all paintings do. And yet it also creates the illusion that the viewer is able to participate in the process of painting—an effect I find to be strangely soothing. By immersing myself in the time and place in which Rembrandt produced this image, it feels as if some of his energy is being passed on to me; I'm suddenly motivated again, capable of pursuing my work with the same concentration and purpose he once did. I feel a positive urge to write. It's not only Rembrandt's discipline that rubs off on me, however; it's also the libidinous energy his painting emanates. It's hard to describe the joy I get from examining its surface—a sea of earth tones, smeared almost to the point of abstraction. The brown paint envelops everything, triggering a regressive desire to wallow in the mud. Even the simple robe Moses wears is earth-toned. By choosing these colors, Rembrandt seems to be pointing to the origin of their pigments, their connection to the earth. The only thing standing out from all the brown is Moses's head, which glows like an illuminated panel; his expression seems impassive, however, and is captured in correspondingly dull tones. His shadowy gaze amounts to a symbolic rejection of the idea that this painting should be perceived by the eye alone: It feels like you're supposed to touch it. I'm also fascinated by the way the painting's haptic qualities are offset by its use of text, in the form of the Hebrew letters on the tablet; the painting "speaks" through the tablet, at least to those who can read Hebrew. And yet it also seems as if Moses wants to hurl the tablet at anyone who, like me, is standing in front of the painting—he's clearly furious that we're still worshipping the golden calf. Moses's relationship to the law is an ambivalent one in Rembrandt's depiction. He holds the tablet high, as if affirming the power of the laws it displays, but he's also visibly struggling under its weight, on the verge of throwing it away and freeing himself of its power. Rembrandt's painting captures the despair of being subject to a law: While we see Moses forcing his (imaginary) counterpart to respect the commandments written on the tablet, it's clear he also wants to cast them off. With his illuminated head and sprawling gestures,

Rembrandt's Moses has an exaggerated theatricality that I find to be entirely fitting—it's precisely this emphatically staged quality that makes the painting so believable and stirring. Having lost myself in the painting for several hours, I feel a renewed sense of vigor about my own work. My anxiety has vanished completely.

The speech therapist calls. She tells me that she's unwilling to continue working with my father because he refuses to cooperate, treating her with outright hostility and appearing seemingly uninterested in improving his condition. She's also unsure how much he actually understands, and whether the exercises are really helping. As soon as she enters the room, he starts gesticulating wildly, trying to drive her away, and so she doesn't want to do the job any longer. She's given up on him, which sounds like a death sentence to me. He won't live long if he can't speak or swallow. I read somewhere that feeding tubes always lead to complications: They frequently get blocked, which can lead to pneumonia. His days are numbered, then. I do my best to persuade the speech therapist to carry on working with him, but she won't be swayed. I phone my siblings to let them know about this new development. And with this, our hope that our father would make some sort of recovery evaporates.

Thankfully, it's time for my therapy session. Frau Dölling tries to get me used to the idea that the drama with my father won't end well, however hard I fight against it. It's difficult for me to accept that I'm no longer able to do anything for him; should I try to find another speech therapist, perhaps, who might get a better reaction from him? I can't and won't give up on him. But I also realize that I'm totally exhausted; the separation from Antoine had already left me physically drained, and now I immediately have to deal with letting go of my father too. My everyday life also carries on as normal, with an endless list of professional commitments to be attended to—a stack of unfinished paperwork now sits upon my desk, making me feel even more depressed. To top it all, my bank adviser calls me just after my therapy session has ended, hoping to convince me to open a fixed-rate account. This would freeze a portion of my modest bank balance for an agreed period so the bank can use it, and in return, I would receive a fixed rate of interest. The opposite was the case just a few months ago, when those lucky enough to have more than €100,000 in their accounts (unlike myself) actually received negative interest on their balances—and anyone who refused to pay faced having their account closed. The situation has reversed since then, and giving the bank control of your money for a certain period now earns you 2 percent interest on it. But such things don't appeal to me, and my balance is far too low in any case—I don't want to risk suddenly having no money because it's stuck somewhere. The adviser wants to send me some documents to look at and asks if I can give him a good rating in a customer survey the bank recently initiated; only if I give him nine or more points out of ten will my rating be deemed positive, he says. The pressure these bank employees are under is unbelievable. He even tells me that his job depends on my rating. Could he be on the verge of being fired and in urgent need of some last-minute positive feedback from a customer? I postpone filling out the questionnaire and turn to my other duties: answering emails, organizing paperwork, and writing to-do lists. But I'm unable to distract myself from thinking about my father, whose crooked features repeatedly emerge in my mind's eye. His face looks gaunt, and his expression suggests he knows death is imminent. He looks at me, aware that he'll not be in this world for much longer. I decide to go swimming, which always helps in these sorts of situations. I need to swim fast and wear myself out, then my stress will fall away after a few laps.

A few days later, I'm standing on platform 8 at Berlin's main station waiting for the train to Hamburg. Climbing the stairs to this platform always makes my stomach cramp, but I sense this visit will be a particularly difficult one, since my father is now living in a care home that Susanna chose for him. Like me, he suffers from extreme sensitivity to noise, and yet she picked a facility on a busy road for him, of all places. I share his suffering; I so wish I could spare him this experience. Riding along the shore of Lake Alster, the tension becomes unbearable. I wish this train would never arrive.

When I enter the care home, I instantly notice how the noise from the street reverberates inside. This building has no sound insulation. While it looks bright, friendly, and modern from the outside, you only need to walk through the narrow glass door at the entrance to realize that its residents are living in a sort of purgatory. It smells of feces, and the entrance area and hallways are full of disoriented people sitting around in wheelchairs; some drool, while others whimper or talk loudly to themselves. I pass through the lounge, where a couple of residents and a carer sit in a circle, singing children's songs together. I ask myself why such institutions encourage this sort of regression in older people—does treating them like children make them more willing to endure the infantilization this place demands of them?

I open the door to my father's room to find him lying face down on the floor. He must have fallen out of bed. Or was he trying to escape? Panicked, I call for help, and a young carer appears who eventually manages to heave my father back into bed with the help of a strong colleague. No one knows how long he spent lying there on the floor. He didn't hurt himself, thankfully, but he seems resigned and absent-minded. The carer explains to me that she's just a badly paid temp and not able to constantly check on the patients; since her job requires her to regularly move between workplaces, she says she often doesn't get to know those she's caring for at all.

My father suddenly starts waving his arms. He points at his feeding tube and seems agitated and distressed. Seeing that the tube has become clogged, I call for help again, and two carers come and examine it more closely while I wait outside. They eventually tell me my father has a fever and has to be taken to the hospital. I go back into his room and try to reassure him. He looks like a frightened animal. A team of emergency physicians arrives, and I'm asked to leave the room again. He's wheeled out on a stretcher some time later. I follow him and the doctors through the hospital, but I'm not allowed to travel with them in the ambulance waiting outside. My father's mood has shifted radically: He lies on the stretcher beaming, seemingly relieved and happy to be escaping the hell of this care home. I call a taxi to take me to the hospital, where I immediately make my way to the intensive care unit. I see a nurse approaching me, holding the hand of a severely emaciated young woman who's barely able to stand. She's clearly in the final stages of an eating disorder. Death stares out at me from the young woman's gaunt face, and I try to avoid looking at her.

My father receives better treatment here than he did in the care home, however: He's been diagnosed with pneumonia, and they've given him the appropriate medication. It seems his feeding tube was probably blocked, which caused the formula to flow into his lungs instead. The head nurse tells me there are no grounds for optimism, and that my father will die soon. I'm only allowed to stay with him for a short while. He still seems agitated, and I try to calm him down by holding his hand and telling him that he's not alone—I'm by his side. He lifts his arm as I'm leaving, as if offering a final farewell. This image of what may be my father saying goodbye to me for the last time is one I'll never forget.

I buy my usual reading material at the station on the way back to Berlin—a mix of newspapers and lifestyle magazines—but I'm so agitated that even concentrating on *Gala* is beyond me at this moment. My head is filled with one anxious vision after the other: What will happen to me, I wonder, without a life partner and now with a dying father, who, for all his problems, always offered me a degree of protection? While I'm lucky enough to still have my mother, my siblings, and my friends, I feel lost and vulnerable, left entirely at the mercy of my own situation. Is getting support from the men in my life the only thing that counts? Why am I so dependent on them?

    I bump into an old acquaintance in the dining car—a musician who left his wife and child in Hamburg and now lives in Berlin. He's just returning from a visit with his daughter. He talks at me without stopping. I often encounter his type in my social circle: men who see themselves as sensitive and open-minded but always have to have the last word. Like them, he always knows better and is essentially uninterested in me. He delivers an endless monologue without asking me a single question, and the only way to introduce my own perspective is to interrupt him. This dynamic of being forced to fight to make myself heard is familiar to me from countless conversations with male colleagues, and I'm sick of it. Like many of them, this musician sees himself as a feminist, yet he refuses to acknowledge any woman who might meet him on equal footing; his girlfriends were always below him intellectually, and they would inevitably end up punishing him for his dominance by leaving him. These rejections only made him more self-centered, however, and he now sees the world as revolving entirely around him. Listening to another person is clearly torture for him, as he impatiently waits for the moment it's his turn to speak again. Other people are merely sounding boards to him—the idea that they might be able to influence his opinions or perception of himself seems out of the question. His armor-plated ego also shields him from all emotions: Nothing gets through to him, and he essentially reveals next to nothing about himself. We discuss our sleep and money problems, but he speaks entirely in clichés. While I don't want to cast doubt on his claim that he also suffers from sleepless nights, he seems to use his neuroses as a trump card that allows him to play the damaged subject. The more effort he makes to portray himself as a wreck to me, the clearer it becomes that he is actually doing quite well. He tells me of a female friend of his in Berlin who has a serious drug problem and is currently in a rehab clinic. It's obvious how much he enjoys playing the superior role in their relationship: By pathologizing his friend in this way, he cements his dominance over her. While his concern for this young woman could seem touching, the fact that he paternalistically refers to her as his "enfant terrible" is evidence of a glaring asymmetry in their relationship: He plays the role of the caring father figure, while hers is that of the indomitable free spirit who depends on him. Spending time with this musician makes me realize how much I despair at many men of my generation. If I'm honest, I can barely stand some of them; either I feel like a nurse in their company or I have to put up with their lack of self-reflection and unwillingness to abandon their old dominant behaviors and sexist attitudes toward relationships.

It dawns on me that I have barely any prospect of finding a new partner when I'm neither willing to subordinate myself nor interested in taking on the mother role in a relationship. There are exceptions, of course—not all men fit these patterns of stereotypical behavior. I have to stop imagining myself as somehow superior to them; I'm guilty of stereotypical behavior myself at times, for one thing, and for another, I bring plenty of problems of my own to any relationship. I'm a tough case myself. And yet I still find myself wondering if I should give a younger man a try for once. Younger men were often raised by more confident mothers and feel less threatened by partners on their own level as a result. They're also more likely to have experience with therapy, which ideally makes them more suited for a healthy relationship. Then again, how suitable am I? My whole life, I've had nothing but dysfunctional relationships that ended in disaster. Instead of making questionable generalizations about men, then, perhaps I should "turn the lens" on myself, as the psychologist Esther Perel suggests in her podcasts. It's not so much other people who are the problem but me.

For weeks now, I've been toying with the idea of buying some new (and unfortunately very expensive) boots. I found a fantastic pair online and can't stop looking at them, despite the fact that I can't actually afford them. I use pseudorational arguments to convince myself of the objective benefits of these boots, telling myself that the confidence they bring me will soon pay off financially. Only if I wear them will money find its way to me. They're also comfortable and good for the feet, since they're made of soft leather and don't pinch. I found them on an online fashion site several weeks ago, and they've been on my "wish list" ever since. Knowing I can immediately return them if I don't like them makes buying them even more tempting—it's often been enough for me to try certain items on at home in the past, after which I sent them back. I'd already had them.

Making a purchase proves to be all too easy online, where it only takes a few clicks—the whole process is so abstract that I'm able to ignore how much is actually being booked from my credit card. I do my best to downplay the fact that badly paid warehouse workers have to pack these boots, and that the drivers who subsequently deliver them are no less exploited. My enthusiasm for these boots means I'm also willing to overlook the massive carbon footprint transporting goods between countries produces. Since they're only available in my size online, my only option is to order them for delivery; in just a few days from now, my doorbell will ring, and I'll instantly tear open the carefully prepared package and try these new shoes on. I know from experience that I'll feel ambivalent about this situation, exhilarated at wearing these new boots on the one hand, ashamed of my own extravagant tendencies on the other. Once again, I'll chastise myself for living beyond my means—I deck myself out as if I had money, deceiving myself and everyone else. As with so many other items, I'll impulsively sling them into the farthest corner of my wardrobe, so that I'm not constantly confronted with this evidence of my own profligacy. But I'll soon retrieve them, and I'll joyfully strut around in them. While I'll quickly realize that they, like other fashion items, do nothing to fill the emptiness inside me, I'll repress this insight; the joy I feel will carry me away from my feelings of negativity, and I'll be better equipped to deal with everyday life as a result. Wearing these boots will feel euphoric, and I'll enjoy life more in them.

I just found a letter with my "pension forecast" in my mailbox. I quickly skim over it, planning to immediately file it away and strike it from my memory as quickly as possible. But a figure printed in bold catches my eye: €1,500. If I retire from teaching at sixty-five, that's how much I'll get after taxes each month. I can't live off that. I either need to find some other sources of income by then or start saving regularly and build up a reserve. The prospect of having to juggle and work more than ever when I should be relaxing and enjoying life makes me break out in a sweat. Will I even have the strength for it? The best thing would be to start looking out for new jobs now. I resolve to make earning money the focus of my efforts in the future. While I hate to think that this will come at the cost of my writing, I have no choice if I don't want to end up having to keep track of every cent I spend and constantly consider whether I can afford every little thing. My writing would take a back seat then, which would be a tragedy, since intellectual work has always been my passion. Why have I spent years ignoring the warnings in the media, urging me to plan for my old age? I recently read one such headline in a magazine, asking readers if they've "put enough away" for their retirement. While I felt as if I'd been caught out by this question—of course I haven't—I instantly banished it from my mind. It was simply too frightening, and so it had to be driven away as quickly as possible. I spent years wrongly believing that aging wouldn't affect me while probably also assuming that I'd somehow magically end up wealthy. I have my father to thank for this illusion. He's the one who instilled the idea in me that I'm a princess, entitled to a life of luxury. He let me and my siblings spend years thinking we would end up swimming in money, and so we assumed he would make sure our standard of living never dropped. He taught me that living a life of luxury is possible if you only dare to claim it. And with his expensive holidays, Porsche, and sailboat, his lifestyle always seemed more attractive to me than the comparatively modest existence of my mother, who never lived beyond her means. In truth, my father's fortune was always fragile: He created a dreamworld for himself, and I followed him into it. Now this illusion of wealth has evaporated in the face of the news about my pension, and I'm starting to panic. Facing this reality also means taking a realistic view of my father—no easy task, given his current condition.

As so often these days, I turn to the internet for help. I find a meditation exercise for dealing with money worries. The meditation guide introduces the session with a series of relaxing breathing exercises, after which we're told to locate the situation that we're anxious about—having far less money at sixty-five, in my case—in a specific part of our body, and to associate it with a particular color. Mine is yellow and sits in my lower abdomen. Finally, the guide advises us not to become emotionally fixated on money. It won't work, he says; it's better to remain true to yourself, and to focus on your strengths. Opportunities to make money will then come automatically—all you have to do is grab them. I ask myself whether there might be a gendered element to this mantra, since nothing in my life has come of its own accord. I had to ask or fight for everything, including my father's financial support; even my author's fees aren't paid without me chasing them up first. While the meditation guide sees a stoically passive attitude as the answer, I think this would only lead me to ruin—there might be some alpha males whose confidence and composure are rewarded with floods of money, but mine certainly aren't. Then again, I've never really been able to rest within myself; on the contrary, it always feels as if I have to prove my worth to others. Perhaps it's due to the pressure I feel inside that money evades me, then, and not because I'm a woman.

My father has been admitted to a hospice. The doctor who has been treating him told me on the phone that he's unable to do any more for him, and that his condition is too serious for him to be transferred to a care home. The only option was to move him to a hospice—a place where terminally ill people are supported at the end of their lives. In my eyes, hospices are businesses that actively manufacture death, since any stay at one inevitably ends in your own demise, even if this experience is softened somewhat by the palliative care they provide. My mother tells me she accompanied my father to the hospice in the ambulance this morning, since Susanna (supposedly) had no time to do so herself. I ask her how he seems to be faring as he nears the end, and she tells me he seems relaxed, relieved somehow. He's probably happy that his stay at the hospice will soon free him from his suffering.
    I decide to catch the train to Hamburg immediately. Standing on platform 8, the knot in my stomach feels even tighter than last time, and I have to make repeated

visits to the train toilet once I've boarded. The more time I spend picturing the situation at the hospice, the greater my fear of this place of death becomes: By taking this journey, it feels as though my own end is also closing in on me.

Once I've arrived, I spot an opulent Advent wreath at a flower shop in Hamburg's main station. My father has always loved everything to do with Christmas, and since the first day of Advent is just around the corner, I buy the wreath for him. Its thick candles and elaborate embellishments make it unbelievably heavy, and I drag it to the dying man's room as if performing a penance. The wreath symbolizes my father's earlier life, and I hope it will bring him some joy. He's lying in bed, dozing in and out of sleep after a dose of morphine; his breathing is extremely slow, and his breath sounds rattled, but he doesn't seem to be suffering. I'm not sure if he's even aware of me or my gift. A nurse comes and tells me that lighting candles is forbidden for safety reasons—it's fitting that even the wreath is robbed of its light in this death zone.

    I ask her how long she expects him to live; she gives him around two to four weeks. I also want to know if high doses of morphine might not weaken his heart and put him in a sort of permanent coma—wouldn't it be better if he were at least able to realize when his family is with him? She tersely replies that dosing his morphine is the doctor's responsibility. My brother, Alexander, enters the room. He brought a bottle of my father's favorite wine with him—even if he can't swallow, he can still enjoy the taste of it on his lips, he says. While this is a nice idea, my father isn't awake enough to participate in such an experiment. Maybe next time, we hope. I massage his hands and feet, moisturizing his dry skin with a small sample pot of serum I happen to have with me. He seems to enjoy this treatment, blissfully smiling to himself in his semiconscious state. My brother and I talk over our father as if he weren't even there, discussing whether we should celebrate Christmas with him at the hospice, if he's still alive. We then leave his room briefly to inspect the bleak and sparsely furnished lounge areas, scouting their potential as locations for a possible Christmas party. The hallways are calm and deserted, with the dying all quietly ensconced in their rooms. Death is managed to the point of being practically invisible here. This is probably due to the morphine, which allows the residents of the hospice to gently drift away at the end of their lives. It also makes it easy to forget what an agonizing process dying can be. Palliative medicine takes the sting out of death, and what used to be a dramatic event is a peaceful process here.

After a few hours at the hospice, I catch the train back to Berlin. It's time for my appointment with my therapist. I indignantly tell Frau Dölling about all the things that are currently torturing me: First, my painful separation from Antoine, and now, the prospect of having to say goodbye to my father—on top of which, my pension forecast has triggered massive anxieties about my future. My therapist remains silent, leaving me alone in my anguish. She eventually tells me that I look at her as if expecting that she might be able to free me from my suffering. But she doesn't have a solution to offer, and it's not in her power to prevent me from being unhappy; I have to learn to face reality, she says, instead of always hoping to be saved. Her lack of empathy for my situation makes me furious. For her to simply acknowledge how hard things are for me right now *would* actually help—that doesn't mean I expect her to rescue me, or free me somehow! But the honest truth is that I've spent a lifetime hoping for payback: Ever since I was a child, I've secretly assumed that I'd eventually receive some sort of compensation for everything that I've endured in my life, from my parents' divorce to the humiliations I've suffered in my professional life. I often catch myself thinking that all the stress, anxiety attacks, and sleepless nights will eventually be rewarded—that there will come a moment when it will all have been worth it. But Frau Dölling insists that this moment I long for will never arrive. She says the best we can do is work to ensure our wounds scar over, so we're able to live with them; the challenge is to accept this fact without becoming bitter. I ask her what's so wrong with bitterness when the world gives us every reason to feel this way. Bitterness impairs our ability to act, she says, since it inevitably leads to resentment and ultimately poisons our lives. Convinced by this argument, I resolve to fight my own pangs of bitterness, and to remain optimistic in spite of everything. For nothing I've experienced is unique to me: Death, loss, and failure come to haunt us all at some point.

I meet my friend Sabine, who lost her own parents back in the 1990s; her friends took the place of her biological family from that point on, providing her with the emotional support her parents had once done. She's totally devoted to her friends, and she meets up with one or another of them at least once a day. She and a few of her closest friends recently set up a housing group and are planning to construct a building where they'll live together. While this might seem like a recipe for conflict, she says the whole thing has run harmoniously until now, and that they don't even argue about money. Sabine seems balanced and enviably at peace with herself. I have to force myself not to be jealous of her, and to admire the determination with which she makes her happiness a reality instead. And yet I can't help but compare my future to her own: It seems she'll have plenty of people around her in her old age, whereas I'll be sitting around my apartment feeling lonely. I ask her how she coped with the loss of her own parents. She tells me of years spent in painful mourning when she felt totally lost, and when her despair made her tumble into a series of dysfunctional relationships that only deepened her misery. Two things saved her, she says: the support of her friends, and writing. I decide to follow her example and put as much effort into maintaining contact with my real friends as I do into my work. Friendship and writing both carry high risks and the potential for disappointment, however. Friends can betray you or drop you without saying a single word, which can be extremely painful, as I learned from my recent experience with the art historian. And my writing can also lead me into a dead end at times, such as when

I misuse it as a form of self-therapy. Being overwhelmed by negative feelings often makes it hard for me to pay the necessary attention to style, the logic of language, and the special materiality of words—my "sound" as a writer is particularly important to me. At the same time, it's a relief to be able to put the things that are tormenting me down in writing, since it keeps them at a distance. In doing so, the point is not merely to put myself at the center but to use my literary experiments as a means of connecting myself with others. For by following my own inner voice in my writing, I also reach out to those in similar situations: As specific as the anxieties and money worries I describe may be, my hope is that others will still find themselves and their circumstances reflected in my texts.

Hoping to break out of my obsession with my own anxieties, I pick up a copy of Frank Biess's book *German Angst: Fear and Democracy in the Federal Republic of Germany*, which discusses fear as a wider social phenomenon. While Biess tells the history of postwar West German society in terms of its collective fears and anxieties, he doesn't address how individual fears are transformed into collective ones. I consider the question of how anxieties can be transferred between people, similar to how a virus spreads. Should a friend confide in me about her fear of breast cancer, for example, then this fear grips me too, and I feel a tightness in my breasts; fear is contagious, in other words. At the same time, the shift Biess describes from "outer" to "inner" anxieties in the postwar period makes perfect sense to me: The moment the immediate external threat of war disappeared, space opened up for inner anxieties to take over. Biess also describes how the 1960s saw a "sensitization of the self"; as a result, anxiety became more internalized, with sensitivity and self-understanding only creating more room for our inner fears. Am I also a product of this shift, with my thin skin and susceptibility to anxiety? While my fears are undoubtedly rooted in external causes, they're clearly far less serious than a global war. I could also deal with my anxieties differently—by closing myself off to them, ignoring them, or simply repressing them. I might even be healthier and happier as a result.

I just received the sales figures for my last book from the publisher: eight hundred copies. I'm devastated by this news, as it means I can forget about a reprint. I ask myself whether social media might be to blame for this drop in readership. Could it be that half the world now prefers to scroll through Instagram rather than read a book, or are my books simply no longer striking a chord? I've certainly had the impression in recent years that the only ones still reading are those who also write themselves. Perhaps I should give it up altogether, if so few people are interested. Or I could carry on writing for myself, hoarding the manuscripts away in a drawer. Then again, I could also take encouragement from the fact that eight hundred people have read my book, including some I don't know personally. A small but refined readership. Wouldn't it be better to keep stubbornly doing my best at something I love, in the hope that my books will find their audience, and that this audience will grow steadily over time? I wonder how hype is even generated around a book in the first place—can it really be orchestrated in advance, or is it a matter of pure luck whether a book ends up on the *Spiegel* bestseller list or not? Good marketing is half the battle, apparently—and here I can put some of the blame for the low sales figures on my publisher, since there was no marketing or PR work at all from their side. I'm being too easy on myself here, however. Above all, the fact that my book was a commercial flop is due to the fact that it failed to light a spark with readers; while I tried to ensure that as many people as possible would identify with it, it clearly didn't work. Ultimately, there's no way of ensuring a book meets your expectations as an author—you can't control how others respond to it. I resolve to make peace with the facts of the situation, however unpleasant they may be.

Hoping to cheer myself up, I drop into a nearby gallery where an artist friend of mine is exhibiting her new paintings. I'm immediately struck by how radically the space has changed since my last visit: New walls have been installed throughout, dividing it up into multiple "cubicles" that offer extra wall space and a more intimate setting for studying the works on display. The artist also had a red carpet fitted, which not only complements the reddish palette of the dry pigments used in her paintings but also creates a more comfortable atmosphere. I feel far more at home here without the sound of my footsteps resonating throughout the large exhibition space, which I've visited so often; while I'd usually try to escape its austere atmosphere and brutally glaring light as quickly as possible, the soft carpet makes me want to linger a while. This peaceful space has a calming effect on me, soothing my anxieties. I especially like the way the lighting arrangement adds to this sense of security, with the works themselves lit up theatrically while the rest of the gallery is comparatively dark.

    Like in a museum, I sit down on a bench in the middle of the space and take in the scene, immersing myself in the paintings. They're portraits—quickly sketched figures that resemble avatars, despite the vitality suggested by their red tones: revenants who look at me with staring eyes. The press release for the exhibition informs me that these figures were digitally generated based on templates found on the internet. One detail particularly fascinates me: In these avatars' pupils, the artist painted what they (supposedly) saw the moment they were frozen in time. Their gaze is not fixed on the viewer like I thought, since they're actually following an event that preceded the process of painting. The artist thus endowed these figures with virtual lives outside of the paintings themselves. The way she managed to embed an external world within these artificial characters is inspiring. I think about the contrast between the soberly objective painting style of the portraits and the white splatters of paint on their surfaces: Were these marks an attempt to satisfy the art market's desire for authentic traces of the painting process? On closer inspection, however, it's clear that these white splatters are actually negative prints of real paint spots. Once again, what had seemed vital proves to be a technically generated illusion: These splatters feed a desire for authenticity that they simultaneously reject.

    In addition to the individual portraits, I'm also interested in the group scenes: a group of zombie women in conversation, an avatar brother putting a consoling arm around his little sister. While there's no life in this digital world, nobody is alone either—each of its inhabitants is connected or related to the others in complex ways. Perhaps the artist wants to tell us that an ambivalent relationship to others is the precondition of subjecthood. Even avatars don't live in a vacuum.

    My thoughts are suddenly interrupted by the sound of voices—a collector just entered the gallery. He's known for buying a lot. The gallery staff swarm around him, offering him something to drink and doing their best to encourage a sale. Time for me to leave. While I'm happy for the artist that commercial success seems to be beckoning, the presence of the collector also reminds me of my own place in the social hierarchy of the art world. No one offered me anything to drink. I won't let this spoil my mood, however: I feel better for having seen the exhibition, and who knows whether I would have been able to enjoy it in peace with eager gallery staff surrounding me the whole time. Thinking about artistic practices brings me great joy, and there's still a lot for me to do.

It's extremely cold this morning, so I spontaneously decide to treat myself to a taxi. I'm riding through the gray Berlin streets and studying the tired faces of the passersby when my cell phone rings. It's my brother. He tells me outright that our father is dead. Susanna just told him. I almost drop my phone in shock. How can that be possible, when just a few days ago, he was lying there alive in his bed at the hospice, and we were planning on celebrating Christmas with him? I think about our final farewell, when I felt an urge to leave that miserable hospice as quickly as possible and get back to my normal life. My father clung onto my hand, not wanting to let me go. Perhaps he sensed he wouldn't see me again. I should have stayed with him longer instead of tearing myself away from him. How could I have left him there alone when he was so close to death? I burst into tears, overcome with guilt. Sobbing, I ask my brother what I should do. He calmly replies that we should all travel to Hamburg together, to say goodbye to our father. I don't know if I want to do that to myself, especially since I've never seen a dead body before. Convulsed with tears, I ask him if I should cancel my appointment with my therapist, or if actually I need it now more than ever. I feel incapable of making any decisions by myself—my father's death has turned me into a helpless child again. My brother tells me I should do what's right for me.

The news of my father's death has torn me out of my reality—I've lost the horizon my life has followed until now, and my whole system of reference is unraveling without him. Frau Dölling immediately hugs me when I tell her of the news and how it's affecting me; I wonder whether this might be a breach of professional boundaries, but I'm also touched by the gesture. I pass through the session in a trance, barely registering anything. When I tell Frau Dölling how distraught and helpless I feel without my father, she calmly replies that it's time for me to let go of the idea that someone else will protect me. His death should force me to finally realize that I'm ultimately responsible for myself, she says. Every part of me bristles at this insight—by demanding that I let go of my desire for a protective figure in my life, she's asking me to do the impossible. At the end of our session, she tells me to travel to Hamburg and face reality. So, I leave her office and catch the next train. I arrive in Hamburg to find my siblings waiting for me on the station platform, along with my brother's girlfriend. They're all dressed in black, and my sister's eyes are red from crying. We embrace each other. I feel uncomfortable wearing such colorful clothes when they're all in mourning dress—it looks as if I'm being disrespectful toward my father. It's only when my brother's girlfriend expresses her "sincere condolences" to me that the full extent of what's happened hits me. I no longer have a father. I find myself wishing she would take back her words, as if this would somehow bring my father back to life.

We travel together to the hospice, which is even quieter than usual. As before, my father lies in bed, but his hollow cheeks and waxy complexion give him a mummified look. At the same time, he looks contented—all the strain has disappeared from his expression. We talk about how peaceful he looks, and how he seems to be in a better place now. The nurse tells us the window was opened so his soul could leave. I so hope there's something to her belief that the soul lives on after death. At least then our father's spirit would still be with us. I stroke his face, which feels dry and cold, wondering how I should say goodbye to him. Should I say something to him—talk to this waxy mannequin he has mutated into? I decide to take a photo of him, in case there are moments where his death seems incomprehensible to me. If there are, then I can look at this photo, and I'll know he's no longer alive.

Susanna enters the room. She tells us about his last minutes, which she says were very peaceful—at some point he fell asleep, and then his breathing stopped. We stay with him a while longer, then head to a consultation room to discuss arrangements for the funeral. Susanna informs us she'll be organizing the ceremony herself. Once again, my siblings and I have no say in anything, not choosing the coffin, planning the service, or designing the tombstone. I tell her that I'm planning a speech to say farewell to my father, my sister wants to perform some music for him, and my brother also wants to say a few words. I ask myself whether this might be the right moment to announce my interest in certain items from my father's house. But it seems tasteless, so I put it off for another time. There's a small oil painting—a still life—that I'm particularly set on. It hung in the hallway of our old apartment, and I would often spend hours on end gazing at it as a child. While it has no artistic value, this painting is close to my heart. I'd also like to have my father's watch—an old Cartier—some photo albums, and his beige V-neck sweater, which I'm sure still smells of him. I draw up a short wish list in my head but keep it to myself for now.

Back in Berlin, I meet my friend Christian, a half-orphan like me. His father died young. It does me good to talk to someone who's suffered the same loss as I have, and who really understands how it feels; while others whose parents are still alive can sympathize with me, they can't really comprehend the gaping hole my father's death has left in my life. We also tend to banish thoughts of our parents' deaths for as long as they're still alive, as I know from experience. It's simply not allowed to happen. Our parents were always there, and so we assume they're immortal—the idea that they could just disappear seems completely unthinkable. If they do then die, how we mourn them and for how long depends partly on the relationship we had with them when they were alive: The more ambivalent it was, the more difficult the grieving process will be. In my father's case, he not only left behind chaotic finances but also an ambiguous will, which is currently being checked by a lawyer. I find myself fluctuating between anger and pity, at times indignant that he didn't get his affairs in order and take responsibility for his children, at others filled with sympathy for the martyrdom he had to endure at the end of his life. Hoping to distract myself from such thoughts, I ask Christian about his own opinions on the subjects of fear and money. Surprisingly, he replies that he's never felt anxious about the latter. He has lived his whole life as a gambler, he says, risking it all and somehow always coming out on top; to loosely quote Karl Lagerfeld, he also assumed that the money he threw out the window would flutter back in through the front door. He's never lost sleep over money, since he knows he can always come up with it if needed—it's a knack that's always worked out for him until now. In reality, Christian is one of those friends of mine who always has money. This is probably because of his sense of entitlement: Money is attracted to those who, like him, don't feel the need to be constantly on the lookout for it. I consider whether his positive outlook might have a gendered dimension. For someone perceived as a woman to take a similarly entitled attitude to money would be almost unthinkable, and she would inevitably be labeled as insatiable or greedy—having money still has largely masculine connotations. I can only think of a few women in my circle who have money, and those that do usually turn out to have inherited it. Only in the rarest cases did they earn it themselves.

Unfortunately, I have a tendency to compare myself to women who are far wealthier than I am. At times, this even drives me to buy the same expensive products I see in their luxury bathrooms—while my own bathroom hasn't been redecorated since the 1990s and will never be as chic as theirs, the right hand cream or fragrance still lends it a touch of elegance and luxury. I recently treated myself to a Molton Brown candle, which caught my eye in the guest bathroom of a wealthy collector's apartment and now stands on my bathroom cabinet. Such efforts at upgrading my lifestyle also seem to me to have a slightly desperate quality, however. For they stem from the need to compare myself with others, which the philosopher and psychoanalyst Cynthia Fleury says indicates an inner emptiness: Deep down, she claims, anyone who compares themselves with others is essentially afraid of being a nobody. By buying the same luxury products for my bathroom as my well-off friends, then, am I really just filling a void within myself? As if I were saying: Look, I'm somebody too. If I felt less empty and more at peace with myself, it might not even occur to me to acquire these products. In reality, I think things are more complicated.

For comparing ourselves to others is the basis for developing our own identities—it's only by identifying with others that we become subjects in our own right. The point at which a healthy orientation toward others becomes an unhealthy compulsion to compare ourselves with them might also be fluid. To judge ourselves by their standards can thus be both: an essential and empowering means of forging our own identities, and an eternally desperate and futile attempt at filling an inner void.

It also occurs to me that there would be no fashion without comparison, since fashion feeds on the mimetic desire to look or dress like other people—seeing a great dress on an influencer or a friend makes you want it for yourself. Here, too, the orientation toward others is double-edged: While it supports our development as subjects, it can also take on pathological traits.

I've been talking to my mother every day on the phone since my father died. She's refusing to exercise at the moment, despite me pleading with her to stay fit and healthy for us children. She seems to have lost all interest in life since my father died and now spends much of her time at home. It's as if he's dragged her into the death zone with him—a clear reaction to his passing, despite them having been divorced for thirty years! My father died on her birthday, of all days, as if he were trying to prove how close the bond between them still was. At the same time, this day now serves as a reminder of her own mortality: My siblings and I will continue to celebrate our mother's birthday, but in the future, we'll also be commemorating our father's death.

My friend Anne has suggested that I sign up for a dating app; she says things can't go on this way, and that I need some distraction from my current situation. While I can't face the thought of a new relationship after my horribly disappointing experience with Antoine, Anne assures me that relationships aren't the only thing on offer—you can also just look out for potential affairs, have a few dates, enjoy yourself. I sign up for an app she recommended, even opting for the premium membership, then instantly forget about the whole thing. Every day, I battle the urge to look up photos of Antoine and his new girlfriend online; I don't want to stalk him, but I can't help it. I often find what I'm looking for, unfortunately—they seem to enjoy posing for the camera together, and the internet is now full of pictures of the two of them. No one could deny they make an attractive couple. Every picture I find feels like a smack in the face, proof of my replaceability, and that I was nothing but a trivial episode in his life. The first messages arrive via the app, but I can't bring myself to answer them. My relationships always used to be filtered through my professional milieu, since there were always people in my circle who already knew my potential partner well. There's no such supervision here, however, and it's impossible to judge who you're really dealing with. I decide to refine my search criteria, as I feel it would be better for me in the long term to find a partner outside the art world. This would avoid the potential for our relationship to become an instrumental one—I don't want to be half of an art world power couple who discuss their strategies over breakfast each morning. I narrow my search criteria down to architects and lawyers: I like the fact that lawyers generally have a knack for rhetoric, and architects are ideally creative, interested in art without being directly involved in the art world.

    I'm standing in the stuffy entrance area of my bank, using the ATM. I try to hold my breath throughout, wondering how my bank can expect its customers to put up with this. Perhaps this inhospitable space with its penetrating smell is supposed to signal to account holders that they're no longer important—the only thing the bank profits from now are its investments. A poster with the slogan "There's no feeling like having your own home" catches my eye. It shows a blond hetero couple cozied up in front of the fireplace in their socks; this poster lets customers know that enjoying the comfort of one's "own home" is not for everyone, and that only those with suitably bourgeois style and German surnames will even be considered for a mortgage. I think about how nice it would be to have a home of my own, where I felt secure. In reality, the opposite is the case—I'm completely at the mercy of my malignant landlord. Berlin is full of tenants who, like me, are now realizing that they're trapped, forced to accept endless rent increases and exorbitant fees. Moving is not an option; there's no more "affordable housing" in Berlin, for one thing, and competition is fierce for the few apartments that do become available. Local newspapers now regularly feature photos of crammed apartment viewings, with hundreds of prospective tenants forming long queues down the street. Finding a new apartment is next to impossible under these circumstances, and so tenants get stuck where they are (which is admittedly still better than being homeless). The bank's poster shows that it's well aware that its customers are keener than ever to own their own homes now that renting has become a burden. And yet they fail to mention that massively increased interest rates mean it's now hard to pay off any such loan—hardly anyone can still afford to buy a home these days. Owning your own property is increasingly becoming a pipe dream, then, while anyone looking to rent an apartment is equally fighting a losing battle.

But while there are plenty of reasons to be bitter, there are also antidotes. Fleury, for example, recommends sublimation as a way of avoiding slipping into resentment. By this, she means the transformation of negative feelings into creative work—an act of self-actualization that allows us to escape our bitterness. Putting aside the fact that Fleury is addressing a privileged class of creative workers with this recommendation—we can't all be artists, after all—I find her advice eminently reasonable. As soon as I immerse myself in a writing project, for example, my anxieties have a literary outlet, which makes me immune to pangs of envy or bitterness—I no longer brood over my position, or how I'm occasionally treated unfairly by others. At the same time, all the writing in the world won't help if I don't receive even a little recognition for my work at some point. If barely anyone is interested, it takes a constant and enormous effort not to become bitter; it's hard to keep cheerfully working away when it feels like I'm the only one who attaches any importance to my project. Things weren't always this way. Winning the approval of others was less important in the 1980s and 1990s—above all within the subcultures of the era, as Virginie Despentes describes in her book *Cher connard* (Dear asshole). Those who considered themselves part of the "underground" saw a lack of symbolic recognition as a seal of quality, particularly since their aim was *not* to reach as many people as possible but to communicate with a small and select group of the "cool." Times have long changed, however, and clamoring for likes and followers is now the norm. It's also not enough to have symbolic recognition alone. For your work to be considered significant, this recognition also has to be transformed into commercial success. Bestselling authors like Benjamin von Stuckrad-Barre, for example, would have been seen as a joke in the subcultural spaces of the 1980s and 1990s, but they're now courted from all sides.

I try not to be discouraged by these developments, stubbornly continuing to write. Fear can't reach me while I'm immersed in a text, since I'm too busy listening to its demands—whether it wants to be reworked, improved, or restructured. News of rising inflation or interest rates can no longer immediately reach me; I'm shielded from the outside world. I sink into the sound of my text, quietly reading the words aloud to check whether a particular sentence has the right musicality. But it eventually gets to a point where my bills need to be paid, and I need money. This tears me out of my writing, which doesn't earn enough to maintain my standard of living, and so I turn to other, more lucrative projects, developing strategies for making more money and abandoning my attempts at sublimation. And although Fleury praises sublimation as the antidote to anxiety and bitterness, it should be added that this cure is only effective when creative work is well paid.

It's the day of my father's funeral. Anne has offered to accompany me, thankfully. I'm wearing a simple black wool dress and high, supremely uncomfortable boots that are already making my feet hurt. For years now, I've had a problem with my big toe, which swells up as soon as a shoe puts any pressure on it, and I now put surgical tape on the toe whenever I wear closed shoes. After getting out of the shower this morning, however, I noticed that my toe has become increasingly irritated by the tape; it's red and swollen, and I now limp slightly when I walk, trying to protect it.

Anne and I catch the train from Berlin to Hamburg, where my brother meets us at the station with his car. He drives us to Ohlsdorf Cemetery, a veritable necropolis with its own streets and crossings. The funeral is being held in chapel 13, which seems fitting: an unlucky number for an unhappy day. My father's two surviving siblings stand waiting in front of the chapel, and when they offer me their condolences, I immediately burst into tears— any expression of sympathy confirms his death, which I'm still unable to accept. Sobbing, I tell them that I won't make it through the service.

I take a seat in the front row directly in front of the altar, next to my siblings, their partners, and my mother. My father's brother is a Catholic priest and will conduct the ceremony. I never liked him, since he has a tendency to be cynical and is prone to giving resentful speeches. He used to put up young men in his rectory, referring to them as his "charges." His relationship to them was unclear, and there was an air of abuse around the whole situation. The sight of the coffin standing in front of the pulpit is unbearable for me, knowing that my father is trapped inside. I imagine him slowly but surely moldering away in this box, then burst into tears again—the thought of him being locked away in there is almost too much to take. My uncle tells us about the last time he visited my father in the care home, when he tried to reassure him that all would soon be well. He seems to assume that my father is now in heaven and enjoying the afterlife; I wish I could be as sure of this as he is. He eventually signals that it's time for my brother and me to speak. I've prepared a short speech, which describes the longing I feel for my eternally absent father: The more unreachable he was, the more I idealized him. While I mention all the things I'm grateful to him for, I also speak about the injuries he inflicted on me. The fact that I'm able to deliver this speech without bursting into tears is astounding. I sit back down, and Anne puts her arm around me. Now it's my brother's turn. I far prefer his speech, which talks of our father's passion for sailing; it's more allusive than my own, peppered with subtle hints of humor. At the same time, the tragedy of my brother's life also resonates throughout. He never benefited from a father figure; our father simply never took on this role. My sister plays a piece by Mozart afterward, which moves everyone present to tears. And then it's all over. The pallbearers enter the room, four strong men with an air of menace about them. They're here to collect my father. We follow behind them, holding hands. It's just a short walk from the chapel to the family grave. We arrive to find out that there's still no gravestone for my father, and I ask myself whether Susanna might have ordered one already, despite her notorious stinginess. I hate the thought of him having to lie there under the earth without a name for too long. Supporting the coffin with ropes, the pallbearers slowly lower it deep into the ground. Of all the day's events, this is the hardest for me—the awful moment when my father leaves this world for good. I feel an urge to grab the rope and stop them, but I pull myself together. A trumpeter Susanna booked starts playing a melody—my father loved the trumpet. We begin throwing handfuls of dirt into the grave, but I can't bring myself to look at his coffin lying at the bottom. I sway lightly on my feet, and I can feel a stabbing pain in my toe.

The cemetery has a small café, where Susanna has booked a room for the wake. We find ourselves in a sort of conference room: bare walls, plastic chairs, and a tea trolley with white dishes. The only refreshments on offer are coffee and dry crumb cake—no warm food, no alcohol. It's as if she were trying to take revenge on her dead husband by saving as much money as possible; while my father loved luxury and good food, his wake looks more like a youth-hostel party than anything. A few other relatives have come, as have some of his old friends and colleagues. One of them, a lawyer, tells me that my father was one of the most intelligent people he's ever known. Hearing his words of praise for my father feels good. None of the long-term employees from my father's office are here, however—they weren't invited, as one of them told me by the graveside. They've organized a small reception of their own in another café. I'm too weak right now to confront Susanna about her questionable decision not to invite them. She just does what she wants anyway. But I do ask her at some point if I can have my father's sweater and the still life hanging in his house, and she suggests I come by after the funeral to pick them up.

Thankfully, Anne comes with me. It's the first time I've rung my father's doorbell without him coming through the garden to meet me. It hurts. The door opens a crack, and Susanna hands me the sweater. She says she wants to keep the still life. I insist on taking a few keepsakes, but she refuses to let me enter the house—she says she wants to wait until the will is read before dividing up my father's things. Anne and I turn around and make our way back to the car. I'm stunned that Susanna won't let me into my dead father's house; not only is he gone, but now I can't even visit the place where he spent so much of his time. Once again, the premonition that the things he gave me would be taken away again at some point has proven to be true.

I found a letter from my stepmother waiting for me in my mailbox this morning: my father's will. He wrote it by hand. It hurts to be confronted with the authentic traces of his life. His handwriting is highly dynamic, with a strong rightward slant; while it makes me want to keep reading, I don't actually understand a word of what he wrote. We children are alternately referred to as "reversionary heirs" and "ultimate beneficiaries." What does that mean? I call my brother, but he's equally unable to make sense of it. We decide to look for a lawyer specializing in inheritance law, and we're immediately offered an appointment for that same day at a firm in the suburbs. We're greeted there in the afternoon by a stern-looking older man with a bald head. After briefly glancing at the will, he dryly informs us that we've unfortunately been disinherited. All we can do is file a claim for our compulsory part, or hope that our father's wife dies soon—not a likely outcome, given that she's not much older than we are. I find it uncomfortable to admit to this stranger that I've been disinherited; he probably assumes that the reason we're not getting anything is because we were horribly ungrateful children. I want to flee as quickly as possible, away from this place that offers nothing but bad news. It slowly dawns on me that my father betrayed us—while I never expected much of an inheritance, to have him simply sign his house and everything else over to his wife is a bit much. Most of all, though, I resent my father for making it harder for me to grieve him. For instead of crying over him and mourning his absence, I now have to deal with the immeasurable sense of anger I feel toward him.

I'm so shaken by this new development that I'm barely able to keep going. Having arrived back home, I sit down at my desk with the intention of putting my grief down in the pages of my diary. But for the first time in my life, I struggle to write anything. I sit in front of my laptop, but nothing happens: I'm just not capable of working. I decide to go swimming—perhaps that will help. I make my way to the local pool, where I tear off countless laps at rapid speed, trying to wring the rage and disappointment from my body. While I do actually feel slightly better afterward, I'm still not able to work. The shock of the disinheritance has obviously left me with writer's block. So, what do I do now?

Emptying my spam folder, I realize that a number of men have contacted me via the dating app, eventually giving up when their messages were met with silence. Whole relationship dramas have played out without me knowing it—a few of them even berate me for not responding. Among all the aggressive emails, however, I also find a message from a lawyer, written in the old-fashioned style of a letter. This man seems kind and charmingly old-school, so I force myself to arrange a meeting with him. He suggests we meet at an Italian restaurant near my apartment. When the time comes for our date, I squeeze in a spinning session beforehand and arrive slightly sweaty. I've not dressed up at all—I'm wearing a thick sweater, jeans, and boots. Perhaps I want to find out if this man likes me the way I usually look? He wears an elegant suit and sits waiting at the table, full of expectation; the contrast between our outfits makes me feel underdressed, and I apologize for not having made more effort. He's extremely good looking—I'm surprised that men as attractive and charming as him are dating online. We discuss our respective living situations, and he tells me about his ex-wife and daughter. I like the fact that he doesn't say a bad word about his wife; she was unhappy in the relationship, he says, and so she initiated the separation. His daughter is a teenager and takes turns living with each of them. When I tell him about all the drama going on in my life—my separation from Antoine, the trauma of the disinheritance—I worry that I might be overburdening him. We've only just met, after all, and I'm already offloading all my problems on him. Wouldn't it be better to exercise some caution, and hide my desperation for now? Then again, it might be good for him to know who he's dealing with. I'm not interested in a relationship right now anyway; I can't get involved with anyone in my current state. I just want to enjoy someone else's company for a while—to have a friendly conversation, flirt a little, and distract myself from my misery. He also seems somewhat cautious, and when he says goodbye at the end without asking if we can meet again, I worry that I might be too much for him with all my emotional baggage. But then, the following morning, I get a nice text message from him, thanking me for the pleasant evening and suggesting we meet again soon. His tone is friendly, and he doesn't seem to be expecting anything—I'm happy we met, and I'm grateful to the dating app for connecting us.

I've been trying to write a text on the artist Cosima von Bonin for a few days now, but I can't make it past the first sentence. Getting the opening right is crucial, unfortunately, since it sets the tone for what follows: If the initial sentence doesn't work, the whole thing collapses. The deadline passed long ago—I justified the delay by explaining to the client that my father had died. They granted me another four weeks to work on it, two of which have already passed; I was paid an advance for the text, so I *have* to finish it. Unlike in the past, having the pressure of a deadline is no help this time: As soon as I sit down at my desk, the anger I feel at being disinherited catches up with me. I sit there staring at my laptop screen, but all I manage is a few muddled notes. Feeling the need to escape my study, I make my way back to the pool, where I swim against all the rage and sadness within me. After thirty laps, the tension in my body gives way to a deep feeling of exhaustion. Now I'm too tired to write.

Nights have become torture for me again recently. As if at the touch of a button, I now wake up at 4 a.m., convulsed with anxiety about my future. How will I support myself if I'm not able to work? I can't live off swimming, after all, and yet it's the only activity I feel capable of at the moment. Although swimming and writing do at least have one thing in common: Time stands still during both of them. I try to outsmart my body by keeping up certain rituals (drinking my morning tea, taking regular gymnastics and yoga classes) in the hope that feeling better physically will also soothe my troubled soul. It often feels as if the worst is over during the day, only for the night to show me otherwise. Then I lie in bed awake for hours on end. Meditation stopped helping long ago, and the melatonin gummy bears I bought at the pharmacy are proving equally ineffective—they taste good, but they don't stop me from waking up. While I used to be able to calm myself down by reading at night, it now just works me up even more. I'm unable to fall back asleep, so I just lie in bed not knowing what to do with myself. I often think I should try masturbating, but doing so makes me think about Antoine, which plunges me back into despair.

I forbid myself from looking at the clock, which would only fill me with panic. I stopped setting an alarm long ago; I want to be able to sleep in if I need to, and scheduling an early appointment is out of the question these days. Knowing I need a clear head in the morning makes me even more afraid of not being able to fall asleep. I often sleep until 10 a.m., then wake up totally shattered. My entire day is then spent half-asleep—at most, I might manage to make it to an exercise class. Perhaps I should see if there's a self-help group for people who've been disinherited. It's embarrassing to speak about it with people who haven't experienced a similar situation themselves; I noticed during my date that the subject of my father's will makes me uncomfortable. I mean, what sort of father disinherits his children? Something like that usually only happens when the children have done something horrible enough to deserve it. I worry that people will assume my father's decision was justified, secretly telling themselves they would have done the same if they had such an ungrateful daughter. But I'm equally horrified by the idea that they might see me as a pitiable victim who was betrayed by her own father—I don't want to be a victim, even if I undoubtedly am in this case. The worst thing is that I'm not able to confront my father and ask him what he was thinking. I also don't know how I'm supposed to deal with the fact that I haven't been given a single souvenir of him—not a photo, not a letter. Susanna's still refusing to hand over the items I've requested, and we now communicate exclusively through our lawyers.

I've arranged to meet a colleague, Thomas, who teaches in Zurich and is visiting Berlin for a few days. Since we don't know each other well, I decide to keep our conversation on a purely professional level: I plan to briefly mention my father's death, but I'll keep my separation from Antoine and the news of the disinheritance to myself; it's not good for me to discuss these things outside of therapy, since telling other people about my misery only makes me relive it. We meet in a café, and things get off to a good start: We chat about which new publications we're looking forward to reading, and about recent exhibitions that interested us. Once again, however, I'm struck by the fact that Thomas refers exclusively to his male colleagues in our conversation. Listening to him speak, you might think that art history was an exclusively male field, which isn't the case: Not only are men actually in the minority, it's women who are currently doing the better, more original work. Trying to be polite, I ask him at some point about what he's working on at the moment. He waxes lyrical about his various projects, with his new book on the revived role of the "avant-garde" in the art world singled out as a particular highlight. I suggest a few publications that might be helpful for his research and ask him a few interesting follow-up questions. He speaks for half an hour without pausing for breath. I naturally assume he'll ask about my own work in turn at some point, but nothing of the kind happens: He never asks about what I'm working on, and he doesn't mention my most recent book even once. It feels as if my own work as a critic had simply been blotted out: Is his silence malicious, or does it simply not occur to him that I might also have something relevant to contribute? Thomas doesn't seem to register how insulting his lack of interest in my work is; all that matters to him is what his male colleagues do, and so it wouldn't even occur to him to refer to my research. I briefly consider telling him how irritated I am by his dismissive attitude, then decide against it. Commenting on his lack of interest would only make me appear even weaker in his eyes. By simply brushing it aside, I probably appear more confident—like someone who already gets enough recognition and doesn't need his approval. As if I were above it all. The reality is different, of course, and I leave my meeting with Thomas feeling even more dejected than before, asking myself whether I should use this writer's block as an opportunity to take a break, since barely anyone seems to be interested in my work anyway.

I'm sitting in my therapist's office, lamenting my life. Once again, she advises me not to fall into bitterness. We have to carry on, she says, with all of the scars life leaves on us; while these scars can heal, they stay with us throughout our entire lives. I find this prospect fairly unpleasant—I'd rather cast off all the negative experiences that have burned themselves into my body and soul than carry them around for a lifetime. But my therapist says they're now a part of me. She makes it clear that constantly feeling like I'm being mistreated will lead me nowhere and suggests I put my grief about Antoine and my father down in a book. Refusing to give up my defeatist stance, I tell her about my writer's block. She's visibly unimpressed by this: The block will pass, she says, and happiness will return to my life. I don't share her optimism, however, particularly with regard to my future happiness. I find it hard to see myself getting involved with someone else after my disappointment with Antoine. Love scares me. I can't open up to someone again—the risk of being hurt is just too great. I tell her I've resigned myself to life as a singleton. She shoots me a sympathetic look, then quietly replies that I have no way of knowing what the future will bring. I still have a large part of my life ahead of me.

Anne calls. She had a nasty fall in the bathroom and now has a complex fracture in her arm. Her bones split apart like dry twigs, she says, and the doctors determined they're unusually porous. She's now being tested for osteoporosis in her mid-fifties. I visit her at home. Her arm is wrapped in plaster, and she can barely move it. She's in pain. After helping her undress, I run her a bath. I scrub her back for her, then go grocery shopping. Anne now requires help, so a carer will come by each day. Since she's no longer able to carry out her job as a physical therapist, she's condemned to do nothing—not an easy situation for her. We discuss how these new restrictions are a foretaste of old age, when our bodily autonomy gives way to dependence on others. Anne says it feels as if she mutated into a helpless old woman in the few seconds it took for the accident to occur. It's uncomfortable for her to need help performing even the smallest tasks—she can't even do up the zippers on her clothes on her own anymore. She's an invalid before her time, if you will. This only fans the flames of my own anxieties, of course. I'm terrified of old age, and of any sign that my body might be starting to decay: Every new wrinkle on my face fills me with fear, and I often don't even recognize my visage in the mirror in the morning—my features look slack and saggy, and my laugh and worry lines are getting ever deeper.

I avoid looking in the mirror in the elevator in my apartment block, quickly turning my back on it and saving myself the sight of my own reflection. By avoiding being confronted with my own aging face, however, I'm also able to convince myself that I still look like I used to, when in reality I'm long overdue a radical makeover. Anne has regular Botox injections in her forehead and recommended her dermatologist to me; since I don't want to look permanently angry, I'll make an appointment with him soon to have him smooth out my own forehead. Anne also swears by facial gymnastics, which train the muscles in the face. I'll try that too. Nip it in the bud! Delaying the outer signs of aging is also a question of money, however, since these treatments are all extremely expensive and have to be regularly topped up to remain effective; if you don't want to look older than everyone else, then you need to come up with the money somewhere. Money becomes more important as you get older, and especially when you reach the stage where you're not able to live alone any longer. The rich can afford private carers who visit them at home in such a situation, but the rest of us are shoved away in retirement homes or care homes. The treatment you receive in the hospital also depends on your insurance status. My father, who didn't have private insurance, was released from the cardiac unit at the earliest opportunity and sent to a hideous care home; had he been more profitable for the hospital, they probably would have taken better care of him.

It's time for another evening out with the lawyer I've been flirting with online. He suggests we meet at the Italian restaurant again. We get on well; the date flies by, and I can feel myself perking up a little in his company. There's a curious moment when the time comes to settle the bill, however. He insists on paying—an old-school move. But then our waitress comments how nice it is to see him again, with a smirk that makes it clear I'm not the first date he's brought here. I'm one of many, then. With this, my naive belief that there was something exclusive about our relationship evaporates and is replaced by the realization that, once again, I'm actually entirely replaceable. This is the nature of dating apps, of course—you're in competition with others. I go to the bathroom and quickly visit his profile, which I never actually looked at carefully until now. On closer inspection, he does actually seem to be a bit of a Casanova, with his gelled-back dark hair and tanned skin. He's a womanizer! When he offers to drive me home, I graciously decline—I don't actually know this man, after all, and I'm certainly not getting into a stranger's car! I ask the waitress to call me a taxi, and on the way home, I decide not to see him again. I don't want to be one option of many, and I don't need to convince him that I'm better than all the others.

 If I'm honest, my own behavior in my younger years wasn't much different from his—I always had a few potential flirts lined up, even when I was in a relationship. My mother had already been abandoned by multiple men by then, and I was determined to avoid the same fate by any means necessary. So I fostered intensive relationships with other men in case I found myself unexpectedly single, going from one relationship to the next and never spending a long time alone as a result. Things are different following my separation from Antoine, and there's no one waiting to take his place. This might be partly due to my more advanced age, since potential admirers tend to go for younger women. Then again, perhaps I simply give off the wrong aura—that I'm just too miserable to flirt.

I swore after Antoine that I'd never be with another man from the art world. That's why the lawyer seemed so promising: He comes from another milieu and isn't interested in my (supposed) social status in my own social universe. This could ideally mean that he likes me for who I am. At the same time, dating within one's own context also carries certain advantages. I usually had a rough idea who I was dealing with when I dated men from the art world, as they'd already gone through a sort of screening process, whereas the lawyer remains an unknown quantity to me: I can't classify him, and that scares me. If he helps me into my jacket, for example, then I might appreciate the old-fashioned gentlemanly gesture, but it also makes me question whether he's firmly stuck in the patriarchy—an old-school man who needs women to depend on him in order for him to find them attractive. I can't take any more uncertainty in my life at the moment, and certainly not in the form of a shadowy stranger. I've got enough on my plate crying for Antoine and grappling with all the contradictory feelings my father's death has brought up in me.

My toe is now so swollen that I'm only able to wear flexible sneakers. The situation has become urgent—I need to find an orthopedist, and I might have to consider an operation. While it might sound laughable, the thought of not being able to wear shoes with heels anymore fills me with anxiety. I need the extra height they give me to feel confident in social situations; I can't imagine going out or giving a talk in worn-out sneakers, and flat shoes make me feel small, like I might be overlooked. Heeled shoes are like crutches that my self-confidence relies on. Now panicked, I search online for orthopedists specializing in foot problems (most of them are men) and make an appointment.

I'm sitting in the overfilled waiting room of a surgeon who specializes in feet. The majority of those present have mobility problems—some walk with a stick, while others grunt and groan with every movement. It takes a long time for my name to be called, and at one point I consider leaving, since my own problem seems minor in comparison. After briefly looking at my toe, the doctor orders me to get it X-rayed. He eventually informs me that I have arthritis in my interphalangeal joint. It's rare to find this problem in this part of the foot, he says, and so he can't say for sure whether an operation would help or not. He writes me a prescription for shoe inserts, despite the fact that this will only reduce the amount of space in my shoe and squash the toe even more. I leave the clinic downcast, resolving only to buy slightly oversized shoes in the future. Perhaps then my poor toe will have some peace.

Back at home, the doorbell rings. It's the postman: He has a registered letter for me and wants to come up so I can sign for it. I flinch at this, since I'm still in my pajamas and not presentable at all. I also fear the worst: Could this be the news I've dreaded for so long—that my landlord is finally kicking me out of my apartment so he can use it himself? I wait by my door, trembling with fear. But when the postman hands me the package, I'm astounded to see it actually contains six paperbacks: It's the Spanish translation of my last book! I can barely contain my joy, and I notice how I instantly feel calmer. The book looks good; I like the cover, and I'm grateful to the translator for making my thoughts accessible to Spanish-speaking readers. I agreed to the translation a year ago, after which I forgot about the whole thing—I'm always focused on the next task, never looking back. I lay the books down on the kitchen table and enjoy this moment of satisfaction. I eventually put them away on the shelf, however, and then it's time to return to the tasks at hand.

I've now come to the conclusion that my being disinherited was actually entirely justified. Why should I be given something I didn't earn myself? The fact that inheritances leave some people better off than others represents a social injustice, after all; it's enough that my father supported me financially while he was alive—why should I get his house too? At the same time, it always stings when others who have also lost a parent tell me how carefully their father (or mother) managed their own estate, making sure it was divided up responsibly between the children. Had my father done the same, I'd find it easier to grieve for him now, since I'd be able to focus on my memories of him instead of my anger. The fact that my biological family was so dysfunctional made me seek out other families in my younger years, hoping to find a model for a happier life. But the more time I spent with these other families, the more the old proverb "in every home a heartache" proved itself to be true: Behind the facade of every seemingly intact family were massive conflicts and a great deal of suffering. In reality, they clearly weren't any better off than I was. And yet I continue to dream of meeting a man whose family will take me in and support me emotionally.

The lawyer wants another date with me. I'm hesitant—I had decided not to see him again—and yet I also feel flattered somehow. I suggest we visit an exhibition at the Gropius Bau together. We meet at the museum. He's wearing a dark brown hip-length leather jacket, giving him the look of a taxi driver from the 1970s. I have to admit that I'm slightly embarrassed by his appearance—he certainly doesn't seem to care about current fashion. I'm still attracted to his physical presence, however; I enjoy feeling him next to me, and I like his skin and the shape and texture of his fingernails. We walk through the exhibition together, and I give him a basic introduction to the artist's practice, pointing out a few works I particularly like. When we've finished looking around, he suggests we visit his fitness studio, where he's secured me a guest pass and booked us a yoga class together. We make our way there and lie down side by side on our mats. I try to hide my swollen toe from him, shooting him furtive glances: He has a dark complexion, isn't particularly agile, and has a problem with his own big toe—the nail seems dead or stunted somehow. Could this be a sign we belong together? The session is too tame for me, and I'm relieved when I'm eventually allowed to do a headstand, which no one else manages. While I'm uncomfortable drawing attention to myself, I'm also slightly irritated by how undemanding the session is. All they do here is sit around and breathe. At the same time, it's nice he thought of it—I've never had a man suggest anything similar before. We go for something to eat nearby afterward, and I'm still attracted to him, still enjoying his physicality. It's time for an honest conversation. I tell him that our relationship has to be exclusive if we're going to carry on seeing each other; while I can feel something developing between us, I say, I can't let myself get involved if I'm going to be constantly worrying that he's meeting other women. He agrees to this pact and asks me not to have any other dates of my own in return. We'll concentrate on each other for now and see where it goes. While I didn't want a relationship, I seem to be on that path. Typical me!

An email arrives, inquiring about a possible catalog text. While I resolved long ago to increase my writing fees, I'm now faced with the question of how I should justify this. I could simply say that I'm charging more for my texts these days, since a lot of knowledge and experience goes into them. The problem with this idea is that there are any number of colleagues who would jump at the opportunity to take on the job for less money; if the client thinks my fee is too high, they can easily replace me in the blink of an eye. By making this request, then, I risk the whole job slipping through my fingers. It's also made more difficult by the fact that demanding more money always makes me feel like a capricious diva—I don't really believe I'm entitled to better pay, since deep down I'm convinced I should be happy if someone wants anything from me at all. I also worry that I won't be asked to write another text if I come across as presumptuous and greedy. And since it could turn out to be my last job anyway, I'd surely be better off accepting than trying to negotiate better conditions. That said, I'm always hearing from my commercially successful artist friends that you have to be straightforward about your needs and clear in your demands—no one will take you seriously if you agree to work for a pittance, they tell me. While this might be true for established artists, it's different for critics: Being poorly paid is a matter of professional ethics for us, since it's expected that we will write purely out of our love for art, without even thinking about money. There's an unwritten rule that you don't discuss financial matters with clients, and so I find it hard to even mention my fee to them. I consider my options: Agreeing to do the text for a low fee will only put me in a bad mood while writing it, and I'll spend the whole time feeling as if I'm being exploited. I could also use this time for other things that might earn me more money. It's not a project close to my heart; I don't feel the need to write about this artist, and so the only reason to do it is for the fee. Gathering all my courage, I draft a response in which I thank the client for his interest and tell him I'd be happy to take on the catalog text. But I also add that I'll be charging higher fees from now on, which I'm sure he understands. I set the price at €5,000 and flinch inside—it's far more than critics usually get for a catalog text. Factor in tax deductions, however, and it sounds like far less—there's not actually that much left. I try to sound confident rather than defensive in my email; it feels pathetic to be grappling for the right words when I'm essentially just asking for more money. As long as I don't really believe that I'm entitled to it, no one will give it to me. I need to change how I think about myself—to build up my confidence and dare to act as if I'm unique and irreplaceable. To let them know: If you want me, then you're going to have to be prepared to pay me more. I put off sending the email for now.

My siblings and I meet at my apartment to discuss the situation with the will. We decide that my brother will file a claim for his compulsory part while the rest of us remain revisionary heirs, keeping our fingers crossed that our stepmother dies sooner rather than later. We agree to divide up any money we do get between us, whether it's a compulsory portion or whatever else is left after Susanna dies. After all, the lawyer reassured us that you can't simply disinherit your children in Germany, and that each of us has a statutory right to a certain share of the estate. Frau Dölling also recently advised me not to put up with my father's betrayal, and to file a claim against Susanna; it's important to put up a fight when we're treated unfairly, she says. While I'm not sure I have the strength to spend years fighting my stepmother in court, having my siblings at my side makes it seem more manageable—I spend all my time worrying about the disinheritance drama anyway, so perhaps it's better to deal with it head on. There are many things I'd rather concentrate on than this unhappy episode, but it has me in check: I can barely focus on my work, and so I end up fleeing to the swimming pool. While there are moments where I'm overcome with outrage at my father's behavior, I have to be careful not to get too used to this feeling: Focusing on my resentment makes me passive, and seeing myself as a victim only robs me of the courage to face life.

Hoping to find some distraction, I arrange to meet my friend Bettina in a nearby café. She's one of the few friends of mine who doesn't work in the art world. She spent years working as a financial adviser for a bank and will soon retire—at fifty-nine. She says she's earned enough to stop working. She bought a small house in the countryside outside Berlin with her severance pay, and she'll live off the income from her investments in the future. I'm fascinated by this, since most people I know have to work for their money, instead of it working for them. I wouldn't even know how to go about making mine work for me. My father always said you should only speculate with money you can afford to lose, and since I never had extra money to play with, I never dared to venture out onto this terrain. Talking to Bettina now, however, I realize I backed the wrong horse by focusing on salaries and fees—I should have consulted her years ago and given her everything I had (which admittedly wasn't much) so she could make more out of it for me. But that ship has sailed now. I'll have to work until my last breath to afford a comfortable lifestyle when I'm older; while Bettina relaxes in her country house and continues to travel, I'll keep on toiling away until I drop.

I wonder if working your whole life might be the price you pay for attaching more importance to symbolic capital than economic capital. Earning money simply wasn't important to me when I was younger; I wanted to spend my time reading and writing, and I felt I had something to share with the world. Why is cultural work now so badly paid that many in the field end up trapped in poverty, while those who invested their money get ever richer? Wasn't there a time when intellectuals were held in far higher esteem by the likes of Bettina, instead of being pitied by them? Earning money from a book has become almost unthinkable, and authors now have to teach and do other jobs if they're to make ends meet. When I ask Bettina if she's willing to help me develop some strategies for earning more money, she says the only realistic option is for me to take a job as an art consultant. While this would compromise my independence as a critic, I might have no choice but to swallow this bitter pill if I don't want to be living like a pauper when I'm eighty.

Susanna has announced that she's selling my father's house; he signed it over to her, so it's hers to do what she wants with. Not only will we children not receive a share of the proceeds, but we're not even getting any furniture or keepsakes. My father spent more than thirty years living in that house, and now the traces of his life are simply being erased. It almost feels as if his existence were nothing but a dream: He was rarely there for me in life, and now the signs that he was ever here are disappearing, just like he used to. His house will pass into new hands, from which point on it will no longer be accessible to us, his children. And at some point, the fact that he once lived there at all will become a faint memory. I hope there's a headstone for him now at least, so that he has a designated final resting place. That it didn't occur to Susanna to give us a few souvenirs of him is unbelievable. She's still refusing to let us into the house—she'll finish sorting his things alone, then draw a line under her life with him. It's fitting, in a way: He was never there, and now he's gone for good. There's no place left that bears witness to his memory.

At Frau Dölling's office, I tell her about my date with the lawyer. She seems uneasy that I've plunged into another relationship so quickly, instead of taking some time to focus on being alone; she says that I still haven't processed the failure of my last relationship at all, and that it's far too early to be pursuing something new. I get the impression that she'd prefer me to continue therapy as a single person. Then we'd have to focus exclusively on me, which I might find uncomfortable; by seeking escape in a new relationship drama instead, I'm running away from the hard work I need to do on myself. I assure her it's not a case of love at first sight, and that I'll take the time to get to know this man before getting into anything serious with him. She asks me what it is that he has to offer me. I'm perplexed by the question, since it never occurred to me to ask anything similar in any of my relationships. I always just got together with men from my circle; they were interested in me, so I gave them a chance, without putting them through any sort of verification process. I accepted them and their situations as they were, without considering what they could do for me or if they were even good for me—asking what sort of benefit they might bring me would have felt presumptuous. Love should be free of such calculations. Although I have to admit in retrospect that I was definitely attracted to Antoine's wealth; if only he'd been as generous with his emotions as he was with his money. While I didn't actually know Antoine had money when we first met—no one could accuse me of being a gold digger—I was happy to accept his lavish gifts and expensive dinner invitations. The lawyer, however, doesn't seem to be rich, but he's probably still fairly well-off. There'll be no holidays in five-star hotels with him, but he'll hopefully be there for me when I need his support. The thing I like most about him is how open he is with his emotions, and that I can tell him about all the things that are worrying or irritating me without having to fear that I'll scare him off. At our last meeting, for example, I told him about my fear of being abandoned. While a lot of men would have run a mile at this admission, worrying (perhaps understandably) that I'm clingy, he listened quietly to what I had to say before gently replying that he'd have to find a way to make me feel more secure. I suggested he start immediately. He could respond more quickly to my text messages, for one thing—he often waits several hours before replying, which I then spend anxiously worrying. He promised to check his phone more often in the future, and to write back more quickly.

 I tell all this to Frau Dölling, who still seems skeptical. When I explain that I'm reluctant to view my relationships in terms of their costs and benefits, she tells me that she's more interested in my self-esteem; I have a lot to offer, she says, and so it's fair to expect that my partner gives me something in return. This entitled mindset still seems strange to me, but perhaps that's my problem: I've never felt like I was allowed to make demands on the men I was involved with. I always felt as if I didn't deserve any better, and that I should be happy that any man was willing to get involved with me at all.

I called my father's number this morning. I just can't believe he's not here anymore. I only reached his voicemail, of course, as always used to happen with Antoine, who, although still alive, has also disappeared from my life. Searching the internet for pictures of my father, I come across a photo of him surrounded by his "business friends"—a group of men (naturally) who regularly meet at a luxury hotel to discuss their work. A cross now stands next to my father's name. I wonder who's responsible for this—who it was that drew this final line under his life. Now he's officially dead on the internet too. Resisting this realization, I feverishly continue looking for pictures of him. I find one of him standing in a meeting room with a client: His face is gray and hollow, and he looks utterly exhausted. The photo was taken just a few weeks ago. Perhaps he'd already reached the end of the road by that point and was just hiding it from us children. I move on to looking for photos of Susanna. Nothing comes up, thankfully, but I do find her name in a list of donors to the Elbphilharmonie concert hall. So that's what she's using my father's money for—to support a cultural institution that's universally treasured by Hamburg's moneyed bourgeoisie. It could be worse.

A distant acquaintance calls. A close friend of hers has decided to start collecting art and is looking for an adviser, she says; would I be interested? After thinking it over for a moment, I tell her I'd be happy for the three of us to meet. Her friend is the founder of a start-up and sold his company for several million, of which he apparently now wants to spend a million on artworks. We meet at a restaurant a few evenings later. He's an eternally youthful type, tanned and cheerful in designer sneakers—a man of success. I do my best to find out whether he's genuinely interested in art or just attracted by the prospect of a good investment. He talks constantly about Gerhard Richter—he'd clearly love to have a Richter painting, but it's not as if I can just magically organize one for him. I suggest we visit a few galleries together over the weekend, and that I develop a concept for his collection beforehand, in view of current exhibitions. He agrees, and so I spend several hours at home drawing up a provisional concept based on our conversation.

    We meet for our gallery tour the following Saturday morning. I pull out all the stops for him, introducing him to a few of the gallery owners and even showing him some works hidden away from public view in private showrooms. He seems to take all this as a matter of course, and he eventually says that he'll need to speak to his wife about any potential purchases, since it's her decision too. So why isn't she here? I leave feeling irritated, after which I don't hear from him for several days. At some point he lets me know via WhatsApp that he's decided to buy at auction instead; the works I showed him weren't what he and his wife are looking for, he says. When I ask him to compensate me for my time, he tells me he considers it to be a normal part of customer acquisition. My mistake! I should have negotiated the financial conditions with him beforehand. Now I won't see a cent, and he'll buy his artworks at some provincial auction based on nothing but gut feeling. A classic lose-lose situation. I chalk the whole thing up as a learning lesson. I should have known from the start that this macho business bro wouldn't take any lessons from me. I sensed during our gallery tour that he's essentially unable to cope with a woman knowing more than him; my expertise threatens his image of himself as the one who always knows best, and so to regain the upper hand, he's now going about it alone. My first mission as a consultant has definitively failed. But I won't let it happen again.

I had a dream last night that I called Antoine to try to win him back. He just asked why I was doing this to myself, then hung up. I woke up drenched in sweat, wishing I could banish Antoine from my dreams. But we don't have any control over our unconscious, unfortunately, and mine still seems to be fixated on him. Meanwhile, my conscious desire has been directed toward the lawyer for some time now—I'll call him Wilhelm here—and our relationship is doing me a world of good.

    We just enjoyed an intimate meal together, and it was lovely. He drove me home afterward—I've dropped that rule now—and we had our first kiss in front of my building! I have to admit that it blew me away—it was the sexiest kiss I've had in my entire life. Not only is Wilhelm a very good kisser, but he's also got a lot of erotic charisma. While I feel increasingly attracted to him, I'm also worried that I'll be overcome with passion too quickly; as I know from my experience with Antoine, passion makes you vulnerable and can quickly turn to misery. Can you have the commitment without also having the pain? Is it possible for me to feel safe and secure in a relationship with Wilhelm? While Frau Dölling told me recently that it's extraordinarily important that we compare the images we hold of others with the reality, experience has taught me that there is no perception of reality that is not filtered by projections. In part, then, my view of Wilhelm is inevitably a product of my own fantasies. But I'm still doing my best to find out who he really is.

    My therapist often brings up Donald Winnicott's concept of "good enough": The important thing is that we find a partner who's good enough for us, she says. I bristle at this, since I've always aimed for superlatives in my life—I want to live with the best and most amazing man, not one who's "good enough." What a depressing thought! At the same time, I do see her point. Having unrealistic expectations of your partner only leads to frustration and disappointment: Either your dream man turns out to be a product of your imagination and projections, or you end up making excuses for a partner whose behavior is, in reality, unacceptable. By contrast, a partner who's "good enough" gives you exactly what you need—no more, no less. While life with them doesn't feel like being in seventh heaven, the realistic nature of the relationship means you can enjoy it unconditionally. The concept actually relates to the mother in Winnicott's work: According to him, anyone with a "good enough" mother is lucky, since it's all that's really possible. I find it hard to accept this idea, even if I agree that excessive ambition and feelings of omnipotence ultimately lead us to unhappiness.

I'm having an anxiety attack (although the French term *crise d'angoisse* comes closer to expressing the level of threat and fear that I'm feeling right now). Wilhelm told me today that he's attending a concert with a friend; they booked the tickets long ago, he says. They met on the dating app, which makes me nervous. Now it's almost midnight, and he still hasn't sent me his usual message wishing me good night. I'm totally distraught, and so I call around friends who do their best to calm me down. Anne promises to come by for breakfast tomorrow to support me. I already know I'll spend the entire night lying awake. While I'm furious with Wilhelm for his thoughtlessness, I'm also angry at myself. Why am I making such a drama out of the fact that he hasn't been in touch, when I could just trust him to do the right thing and get a peaceful night's sleep? But this potential rival bothers me. Perhaps she's made a last-ditch attempt to win him back. You never know. I'm also depressed that my fear of being abandoned is as deep-seated as ever. I feel like I did during my childhood, when I spent many nights waiting for my father to return; since he often didn't come home from his affairs until early in the morning, I would spend hours lying awake in bed then too. How am I supposed to trust a man now, when my father showed me there's every reason not to? I take three melatonin gummies at once, which make me dozy, and I do eventually fall asleep. There's still no message from Wilhelm when I wake up the following morning. Luckily Anne comes over as promised, and we discuss how I can get out of this relationship, which has become so painful for me so quickly. I already feel a deep connection to Wilhelm (unfortunately), but I can't face spending any more nights lying awake worrying—I don't want to be with someone I can't trust. At some point, he does actually call. Everything's OK, he says, he just forgot to check his phone; his companion ended up irritating him, and he'd like to see me. While I can barely contain my joy, I'm reluctant to show it. I need to speak to him and let him know that he needs to be more considerate toward me in the future if he doesn't want me worrying constantly. At the same time, I'm not comfortable demanding that he commit to me: Wouldn't it be better to wait and see what happens between us, instead of demanding he behave in a way that doesn't actually benefit me if it's not done willingly?

Wilhelm got us tickets for the Philharmonie—a performance of Dvořák's *Stabat Mater*. We meet at the main entrance, where he gallantly helps me out of my coat and takes it to the cloakroom. I'm not used to such behavior, and I feel slightly disoriented as I wait for him in the large entrance hall. He comes back and leads us to our seats in the stalls. The hall is full, and there's tension in the air. I sense that many in the audience share my deep-seated shock at the current war in Israel, and at the massacre that occurred there just a few weeks ago. My Facebook feed has been full of obituaries recently, with countless photos of happy young Israelis who were slaughtered by Hamas. The thought of all these young lives being ended so abruptly is unbearable. And now Israeli bombs are killing people, among them many children, in Gaza every day, with no end in sight. I feel truly shaken by all the suffering—my anxieties and money problems seem insignificant in the face of this horror.

    I buy a concert program at the last minute, so I have at least a rough idea of what the piece is about. It's a dirge based on a liturgical text from the Middle Ages, and I'm startled to read that Dvořák composed it as an elegy after losing three of his children. The perfect soundtrack to what's currently going on in the world.

    The performance begins. A member of the orchestra gives a short speech, then asks for a minute of silence in memory of the victims of the massacre and the war. I stand up on unsteady knees, close to tears. The hall is totally silent—the rest of the audience seems to be as moved as I am. Then the orchestra strikes up the first penetrating minor chords, and it's clear that this piece deals with the rawest of emotions: grief, anger, outrage, and despair, all captured in musical form. Fighting back my rising tears, I reach for Wilhelm's hand, craving his support. The voices of the choir become ever louder, and as the piece crescendos to its mournful climax of rage and despair, the loss of my father hits me to my core. The choir's voices ring out as clear as a bell, despite the somber melodies. As if there were a light shining at the end of this tunnel. Might Dvořák's piece be considered the equivalent of Mozart's Requiem, I wonder? The solo singers start their parts, and the mood shifts to one of compassion and empathy. The tenor sings an aria in which he asks God to "drive the wounds of the Crucified deep into my heart." He wants to carry these injuries within himself. Here, empathy is portrayed as something that must be asked for and practiced with humility. I'm particularly amazed by how the piece allows for such intimate and consoling melodies in the midst of these painful tones. At some point, this intimacy tips over into drama, however, and what began as a hopeless lament turns into an ecstatic celebration of the resurrection. Above all, the "Amen" fugue at the end seems to convey an almost exaggerated sense of euphoria, which I see as both the opposite and equivalent of absolute despair: The one defines the other. The conductor prolongs the ending by holding his baton in the air for thirty seconds, during which the entire audience holds its breath. There's a slight pause, then a roar of applause. I clap like crazy, wiping the tear-stained mascara from my eyes and trying to compose myself. Wilhelm also seems moved; he looks softer somehow. The intensity of this musical experience has brought us closer to one another. We make our way out of the hall hand in hand, more connected than ever.

Another dream about my father. We're in a sailboat, and he sits at the rudder, steering us through strong wind and high waves. I'm wearing a life jacket, and my father has tied me to the boat with a rope, so I won't get swept away if it capsizes. The boat lists at a steep angle; waves constantly break over my head, and I'm already soaked to the bone. I ask my father to take me back to the harbor, but he ignores my pleas and sails even closer into the wind. We speed up—the boat's now on the verge of capsizing. My father looks different somehow, as if he'd just come back from the dead: His face is gray and lifeless, and his expression has a demonic quality. I finally scream at him to turn the boat around and untie me. But he doesn't, and I wake up feeling disturbed. Was this dream a parable of my need to be protected, and of my father's inability to provide me with this protection? I'm less irritated by his behavior in the dream than I am affected by his appearance: He seemed tormented, certainly not like someone who's resting in peace. Does this mean he's now burning in hell—that he's being punished for all his misdeeds? For me to sympathize with him even when he's acting abusively is typical of me. He treated me terribly in this dream, after all, chaining me up and putting me at the mercy of his irresponsible actions. But I still loved him. His behavior in the dream was also an exaggeration; he was never really that bad in reality. I want to bring him back to life. It's horrible to sense that his suffering didn't end with his death—that he's running rampage in my dreams because he's unable to rest. I'd like to make my peace with him, but it's hard.

I open my mailbox to find a large envelope. It contains a letter from an artist I haven't heard from in decades, apologizing for her behavior twenty years ago. I'd conducted an interview with an eminent French sociologist whose ideas had strongly influenced my own work, in which I pointed out the "blind spots" in his theory. Astonishingly, this strategy proved effective, since he enjoyed being contradicted and seemed to have a crush on me. In retrospect, I think it was a mistake not to purge this conversation of its slightly flirtatious undertone before publishing it. After the interview had come out, the artist in question published a comic strip in her fanzine—a photoromance of a heterosexual couple flirting, set to the words of my conversation with the sociologist. As if the primary purpose of the interview had been for us to come on to one another. While I tried to ignore the comic and concentrate on my own work, I remember sensing a lot of schadenfreude among some of my colleagues at the time. No one expressed their solidarity with me; on the contrary, they seemed to find the strip downright "funny." It didn't occur to them that the point was to deny me my theoretical interest in the sociologist's work. While this is all water under the bridge, the artist now writes that she never wanted to hurt me. She also sent me the original design to keep. While I'm grateful for the conciliatory gesture, I'm also unsure why it took her so long to realize that making fun of a female colleague in this way might have been unwise. I can't help but think of Jo Freeman's essay "Trashing: The Dark Side of Sisterhood," which discusses the feelings of competition, jealousy, and destructive anger that can arise even among women who are actively engaged with feminism. Why isn't female bonding a thing the way male bonding is for men? Wouldn't it be better if we celebrated each other's achievements, instead of bringing each other down? Then again, it's also possible that my female colleagues at that time saw me as a sort of overachieving monster who could surely take such a bashing in stride. And I put on a brave face, without ever really letting them know how hurt I was.

    I've also experienced a lot of solidarity with women, of course, and I'd never be able to cope with the challenges and problems of everyday life without the support of my female friends. Nor is it the case that I've never hurt another woman in the course of my own career—far from it. Perhaps it's time I apologize to all those I've offended with my own criticisms of their work. I think about all the negative and juvenile reviews I wrote over the years, which I'm sure were insulting for the people in question. Then I draw up a mental list of all those due apologies, resolving to embark on my walk to Canossa soon.

    Could the fact that I get into trouble so often have something to do with my appearance? I used to act as if the world belonged to me when I was younger, as if nothing could touch me. And since I spent every penny I earned on designer clothes, I also looked fairly rich. In reality, I constantly had to negotiate with my bank for a bigger overdraft, and I'd sometimes live off porridge for days on end because I'd spent all my money on an expensive new piece by Helmut Lang or some other designer. Looking back on it now, it's no wonder some people reacted with aggression. But I simply felt better in my fashion armor, since it helped me appear outwardly confident even when I was shaking like a leaf inside.

It's my final therapy session before the break. I tell Frau Dölling about how anxious I felt when Wilhelm didn't write me back, and how angry I am that I'm unable to get my anxieties under control. I recently read another text by Freud in which he describes anxiety as "a reproduction of the trauma of birth"; the "act of birth," he claims, is "the individual's first experience of anxiety," and so it resonates throughout all the anxieties they subsequently experience. To me, this raises the question of how some people can be relatively anxiety-free—they were born, too, so shouldn't they also be plagued by anxieties? I even know a few of these enviable characters myself. Did they just do a better job of dealing with the trauma of their births than the rest of us? Or is Freud's thesis simply wrong?

On the other hand, Freud is right to say that the fact that we experience our anxieties as potentially life-threatening stems from the trauma of our births; if I'm gripped by anxiety, for example, I feel as helpless and vulnerable as a newborn baby.

Talking to my therapist makes me realize that my anxiety is a part of me, unfortunately. It will never fully disappear, she says; the best we can hope for in our work together is that it will be *tamed*. Even if a day comes when I do feel cured, my anxieties will still be lurking in the background. All I can do is try to find a better way of dealing with them. Since any new relationship also poses a new risk of failure, it inevitably leads to anxiety, as "a reaction to the danger of a loss of an object," as Freud puts it. And since the threat that I will lose my lover is a permanent one, my anxiety will always be with me: For as long as I enter into new and intimate relationships with others, I'll have reason to be anxious. In my case, this is aggravated by the fact that I've often experienced object loss in my life. In my childhood, for example, the things that were given to me were frequently taken away again, such as when our beloved holiday apartment on the Baltic was sold following my parents' divorce. We were also forced to move out of the beautiful old apartment we had previously shared with my father. Not to mention my father himself, who was permanently absent, and who I missed enormously. The "fear of object loss" is always with me, then. And, as I go on to discuss with Frau Dölling, the same is true of money. There's a passage in Freud's *Inhibitions, Symptoms and Anxiety* where he briefly addresses the importance of economic factors in anxiety. Anxiety, he writes, is not merely a manifestation of affect but "created out of the economic conditions of the situation," meaning our financial situations alone are enough to generate anxiety in us. Even wealthy people constantly worry that their money might be taken away from them one day.

 I tell Frau Dölling about my longing for financial security, but she claims it's just an illusion; you can have all the money in the world and still be lonely, unhappy, and ill, she says. I respond that not having to worry about money makes things easier if you need an expensive medical treatment, for example. While she acknowledges that having money is an advantage, she says that believing it is the answer to all our problems denies the reality of our crisis-ridden world. Any feeling of security is illusory, according to her. And yet I still secretly hope that I'll earn more money one day, and that I'll end up in a stable and caring relationship. Then again, can any relationship really be stable in the long term? I want to believe it can, and I'm firmly convinced that having more financial and emotional security would make my anxiety attacks less intense. While the idea that my fears are groundless might have value from a psychoanalytic perspective, everything in me resists it. I refuse to believe that my anxieties are simply a product of my ego. And yet it seems as if they are. How can I overcome feelings that are so deeply anchored within me? Perhaps by looking at them from the outside, so they're not able to fill me up and incapacitate me any longer. I think of all my failed attempts at meditating, where the point was always to do just this. I've clearly still got a long way to go when it comes to managing my anxieties. Perhaps I have to experience these fears time and again, in order to learn that they won't actually kill me—while every anxiety attack feels like it could be deadly, I've survived them all until now. Maybe I'll get better at dealing with my anxieties and find these episodes more manageable over time; there's certainly no reason to think my money problems will magically disappear anytime soon, and that my anxieties will just evaporate along with them. How am I supposed to take a relaxed attitude toward money when everything around me tells me it rules the world? Even if I uphold other values, I'm constantly reminded of the enormous importance of money—to deny this would mean denying the reality of social conditions.

    While I need the support of others in similar situations if I'm going to deal with my anxieties better, there's an unwritten law among friends that they won't bother each other with their money problems. Just recently, a friend admitted to me that he's been struggling a bit recently, before adding that he'd spare me the stories of his financial misery. He's clearly embarrassed by his situation and doesn't want to talk about it. Then, a few days ago, I met another friend, whose fingers were totally red and raw, particularly around the cuticles. When I asked how she injured herself, she tersely replied that these wounds were the result of her anxiety; she made it clear that the conversation was finished, and she didn't say another word about her condition. It was obviously uncomfortable for her to talk about the situation, and I didn't want to step over the line by questioning her about it any further. I'm now thinking I should start a conversation group on the subjects of "fear and money," where we could read and discuss relevant texts and talk about our experiences. Discussing my anxieties within a group would allow me to take account of their social dimension while also recognizing their singular nature—by acknowledging that my problems are simultaneously both shared and individual, I wouldn't have to deal with them alone anymore. I draw up a list of potential members and mentally compile a provisional reading list. While forging plans for this group noticeably improves my mood, I know my optimism won't last long, and that I'll be battling panic and despondency again by the time the next bill needs to be paid at the latest. But until then, the hope remains that my life will be less anxious from now on.

It only takes a small thing for my confidence to evaporate. I just heard an interview with Eribon on the radio, on the subject of friendship. He's often been betrayed in his life, he says, and so a few years ago, he asked his closest friends Geoffroy de Lagasnerie and Édouard Louis to sign a friendship pact committing the signatories to absolute loyalty. To me, the contractual nature of this pact is depressing proof that loyalty among friends and colleagues can no longer be taken for granted.

It also makes me question whether my proposed "Fear and Money" group is really the answer to my problems with anxiety. On the one hand, it could help those involved feel less alone, since discussing their anxieties within the context of the group would reveal their social dimension: The group would act as a mirror to their own inner lives, and their fears would reveal themselves to be those of the others too. At the same time, group situations are no picnic—they can even be downright torturous, with their hierarchies, rivalries, power dynamics, and exclusions. The fact that the people involved have different financial situations could also create tensions and conflicts. I myself have ended up embroiled in group dynamics that provided the perfect conditions for my social anxiety to thrive: Certain members (mostly men) dominated, while others (like me) barely dared open our mouths out of fear of saying the wrong thing and being admonished for it. I'd get a queasy feeling in my stomach before each meeting.

As much as I dream of coming together with others, and of opening up to them and getting the better of my anxieties, I also see the risk of such an undertaking. Even if the members of the group agreed to a loyalty pact like the one Eribon demanded his friends sign, who could guarantee they would abide by it? There are also situations where loyalty is misplaced, such as when one member hurts the others with their behavior or oversteps a boundary. I still want to go ahead with the group, since I believe that discussing our problems together will make them easier to deal with. But I have to let go of the illusion that it could be the solution to all my anxieties and money worries. The group is also bound to create problems and anxieties of its own, but at least then I'll have the others to talk to about it. Above all, it's this prospect of sharing my experiences of anxiety with others that makes me feel joyful and optimistic about the group's potential. I start sending out invitation emails to potential members. Should I include Wilhelm? No, I'd rather keep our relationship strictly between us. For us to participate as a couple would also be unwise, since we'd inevitably dominate the group. I send off an invite to a selection of friends, colleagues, and acquaintances who I know are also battling anxiety, suggesting we hold the first meeting on a Monday two weeks from now—a date when the next chapter of my life with anxiety will hopefully begin.

Today is my first birthday without my father. Unlike in previous years, there'll be no one ringing my doorbell with flowers from him, and he won't call—although it occurs to me now that my father actually forgot my birthday for the first time in my life last year. He was unbelievably embarrassed by this when I pointed it out; our birthdays were always sacred to him, marked in thick circles on his calendar, and so he was downright bewildered at having forgotten this important date. I interpreted it as the first sign of his mental decline. And now he's gone. How am I supposed to celebrate my birthday when one of the people responsible for my existence is no longer here?

Wilhelm comes over. He brought me a wonderful bottle of perfume, but I secretly resent the fact that there are no flowers. Then the doorbell rings again. It's a courier with a package: the homemade birthday cake my mother touchingly sends me every year. I take the cake out of the box, decorate it with candles, then place it on the table. While I can't help but wish there were an opulent bouquet of flowers alongside it, I keep this thought to myself. I'm ashamed to feel this way; it's not fair to expect Wilhelm to stand in for my dead father, after all. But a birthday without flowers is no birthday at all for me, and so I decide to buy some myself. I tell Wilhelm I'm going to cycle to the flower shop. He offers to take me in his car, and when we arrive, he buys me a bunch of red roses; while it's a nice gesture, I can't help feeling I've forced him into it. It would have been better for me to have been honest with him about my expectations for my birthday in advance, but we don't know each other well enough for that yet. I also wonder if it isn't a bit presumptuous to burden our partners with such desires. Is my longing for flowers even reasonable? Isn't it time I finally gave up the idea that I deserve to be treated like a princess? I'll never feel as safe and secure as I did when my father would lavish me with gifts on my birthday. He's gone, and my heart is heavier without him here.

I've invited Wilhelm and Anne to a small, intimate dinner at my favorite restaurant this evening; while it feels as if I'm taking on the paternal role by offering to pay, I want them to get to know each other, and I'm curious to see what Anne makes of my new partner. The evening goes well, but Wilhelm has to leave early—he has an important meeting the next day, so he won't be staying with me tonight either. Anne tells me at the end that she liked him, and that he's clearly good for me. When I arrive back at my apartment, I hear the gamer boys in the apartment below me shouting at the top of their lungs; this happens every time they lose a game, making sleep out of the question. I decide to write their parents an email, asking to make sure their sons are at least quieter after 10 p.m., as the law demands. The mother writes back immediately that I should "leave them alone." There's no trace of understanding or consideration. I'm shocked by how aggressive her answer is—what did I do to deserve such a hostile and dismissive reaction? Was my email poorly worded, perhaps? Thankfully, I find a meditation online for dealing with "loud, horrible neighbors"; it's comforting to know that I'm not the only one dealing with this problem. I resolve to carry on being friendly to my neighbors when our paths cross in the hallway. But I'll also keep a record of any noise problems, and if the boys keep me awake too often in the future, I'll hand the matter over to a lawyer to deal with. I might meditate a lot, but that doesn't mean I'm willing to put up with everything.
My friend Stephanie is visiting Berlin from New York and comes by for tea. She's a psychoanalyst and tells me that all of her patients are experiencing an acute phase

of insecurity at the moment. It's comparable to the situation in the 1920s, she says: right-wing populism was on the march back then, too, combined with an economic crisis, high inflation rates, and the consequences of a global pandemic (the "Spanish flu"). On top of this, we now have to deal with a climate crisis that has robbed many of their optimism for the future. Her patients also despair at the fact that there's no end in sight to the war in Ukraine, she says, and that the Israeli army is continuing to bombard the Gaza Strip—they feel powerless in the face of a world whose events seem to be spiraling dangerously out of control. Stephanie sees populist politicians as deliberately sowing further anxieties in this situation, such as when Trump raises the specter of a threat from immigrants then benefits from this same fear by propagating simplistic solutions like the Mexican border wall. Never before has she experienced her patients pouring out so many of their anxieties to her, she says.

I wonder if the comparison Stephanie makes with the 1920s might not be misplaced. The economy was *extremely* depressed back then, the inflation rate far higher, millions had died in the war, and even more fell victim to the flu. Europe also didn't have much experience with parliamentary democracy back in the 1920s. I can't escape the impression that Stephanie herself wants to frighten me with this narrative of history repeating itself. In reality, events never really repeat themselves without deviations and differences, and anything that does happen twice does so in two different contexts. I tell her that I feel her comparison is only useful if it also takes into account the differences between the situations back then and now. I also object to the idea that my anxieties are merely local examples of a global phenomenon: While I agree that individual fears are bound up with shared ones, I insist on recognizing the singular nature of my own anxieties. Stephanie laughs and assures me that she doesn't want to deny me these feelings: "They belong to you, don't worry, honey."

After Stephanie has gone, I look through a pile of invoices I reluctantly pulled out of the mailbox this morning. The local tax office has written to me demanding I pay €20,000 in back taxes; my tax adviser probably declared some payment or other too late, and now I have to transfer the entire sum within ten days. I don't have the money, and I don't know how I'm supposed to come up with it. My father is dead, so he can't lend me anything, and my mother doesn't have the means. Panicked, I run through a mental list of who might be able to help me. I stop on a wealthy collector I know who could easily lend me the money—interest-free, ideally. I write him an email asking if we can meet urgently. It's an emergency, I tell him. Thankfully, he responds right away, inviting me to meet him in his office the following afternoon.
    I put on a girly floral-print dress for our meeting, hoping it will help; while I'd usually prefer to meet him as an equal, playing the role of the helpless female who needs his protection will flatter his ego. He begins by mentioning my father's death, which makes me instantly burst into tears. There's nothing calculated about these tears—in this moment, I really do feel distraught that my father is no longer alive. While his own financially precarious

situation would have prevented him from lending me the money himself, he would at least have been able to give me a few tips on how to negotiate a loan in such a situation; without his advice, my only option is to supplicate myself here. I explain my situation to the collector, and he offers me a loan. He makes it clear that it's not a gift, however, and that he expects me to pay him back with interest in the coming months. Lacking any other option, I instantly agree to this deal, and he writes me a check for €20,000 on the spot.

I feel uncomfortable knowing that I've made myself financially dependent on this man. Deep down, I feel I deserve this money. He should have just given it to me outright, as remuneration for all the years I've spent toiling away as an art critic; he stands for all those people who've made money off the back of my work, after all, and so it's hard for me to feel grateful to him for "saving" me. He's swimming in money. Then again, perhaps the fact that he has not simply given it to me is a sign that he respects me: He treated me like a business partner, and they don't get something for nothing. I could be grateful to him for the fact that I don't owe him my gratitude, then. There's an extremely uncomfortable moment when we say goodbye, however, when he hugs me tightly, and I feel his hand land on my buttock. While I manage to squirm free, it's clear to me that he never would have dared to behave so inappropriately if I wasn't in his debt.

It's hard for me to feel relieved about this tax bill when the price of paying it is so high. I'll have to earn more money in the future, so that I never find myself dependent on the favor of such a character again.

I feel a lot better today: I drew up a repayment plan for my loan from the collector, and in a couple of months, I'll have paid it off and be debt-free. I've also started looking for a new apartment online, since I've decided to move somewhere smaller and cheaper (and hopefully more peaceful). I feel euphoric at the prospect of setting up home somewhere new—the first page of a new chapter of my life, with fewer sleepless nights.

    I also found some inspiration regarding my own future as a writer recently, in Neige Sinno's book *Triste Tigre* (*Sad Tiger*). A powerful account of the incest the author lived through as a young girl, the book is also formally ambitious, intertwining autobiographical account, inner monologue, and direct address to the reader. I was particularly interested in a passage at the end in which Sinno describes the rejection letters she received from publishers after sending them her book. Each of these letters follows the same template: The publishers assure Sinno that her book is exceptionally good, before adding that they'll unfortunately be unable to publish it, as there's no suitable way to market it. My last book was rejected by certain publishers for similar reasons: Their letters always begin with enthusiastic comments, then turn the book down on the grounds that it's not marketable. I think it's probably my previous sales figures that are actually holding them back from taking a risk on me; if they really think a book is good, isn't it their job to find a way to market it? Sinno's book was eventually put out by a small publishing house. It was a great public success, winning the Prix Femina and earning the author a nomination for the Prix Goncourt. Not bad for a book that numerous publishers had written off as unmarketable. I have to admit, this story gives me hope.

It's almost time for my first apartment viewing. While the high number of applicants makes it unlikely that I'll actually end up moving in, I'm hopeful that I'll find a small apartment I like one day. I certainly don't want to stay in a miserable situation just because of the "difficult state of the housing market," as you hear so often these days; I'd rather massively downscale than have to continue putting up with the gamer boys and their noise. I'm meeting the "Fear and Money" group for the first time after the viewing. I'm excited about this, too, with some reservations—the less I expect from this group, the less likely it is to disappoint me. My full calendar of activities—repayment plan, apartment hunting, group meetings—means that recently my anxieties have faded into the background slightly. Is that the solution, then—to simply stay busy, and your anxieties will disappear? Not quite. If Wilhelm takes too long to reply to a message, for example, then I soon feel a knot in my stomach. And "too long" could be five minutes—that's all it takes for me to convince myself he's abandoned me. The only thing that can save me, then, is to get a reply from him. Thankfully, Wilhelm knows about my anxieties, and he's now usually fairly quick to respond. I have to admit that he's trying. And for my part, I'm doing my best not to immediately slip into a panic when I don't hear back from him; after all, my experience with Antoine and my father's death both showed me that I'm capable of surviving even when the thing that I fear most does happen. Both of these men betrayed me in their own ways: Antoine replaced me with someone else, and my father disinherited me. Do we perhaps have to experience the things we fear most? Does immersing ourselves in our fears ultimately help us escape them? It's not that simple, unfortunately. Waiting for a sign from Wilhelm always puts me in a state of unbearable anxiety. The only thing that really helps is a change of scene. And so instead of sitting around staring at my phone and waiting for a message from my sweetheart, I set off for the apartment viewing, with the group's first meeting to follow. While I can't help but take my fear with me, experience has taught me that seeing fear flare up in the eyes of others makes me calmer about my own anxiety. At times I can physically sense other people's fears, whether of their punitive (and imaginary) superego or their failure to conform with social norms. There are even occasions when I meet people whose anxiety seems even greater than my own. It's a comfort to know that I'm not the only one plagued by such worries—no one is alone with their fear, even if it does its best to persuade us otherwise. The truth is it's both—an individual phenomenon *and* a social one.

The apartment viewing is a sobering experience, with fifty potential applicants traipsing through a damp basement that apparently costs €1,200 a month to rent. I make a quick escape and hurry off to meet the group. And lo and behold, our first meeting turns out to be a total success. One participant suggests we actively give ourselves over to our anxieties instead of fighting them, and that we could even write down the negative feelings this experiment triggers in us. Another member of the group objects that money and fear are both phantasmatic abstractions, and that their very nature makes any attempt at capturing them in writing a futile endeavor. We agree that each member of the group should decide for themselves whether to keep a written record of their anxieties or not.

When the check arrives, one (male) member immediately grabs it, saying he'd rather just pay it than have to divide it up between us. While we're all impressed by his generous gesture, it also secures him a special symbolic role within the group: He's now the "provider." We say goodbye, and I set off for home in a good mood—knowing there are others who I can share my anxieties and money worries with from now on feels downright euphoric.

Then again, how much truth can I actually expect from the group, and from myself? Do I really want to reveal my authentic and at times dysfunctional anxious inner life to these people? Isn't therapy the more appropriate setting for that?

Once back home, I start writing up my first notes on "fear and money" for the group. My fear of exposing myself disappears with the first sentence, which seems as if it had been written by someone else entirely. It is not my own voice that speaks here, but a literary one—a fictional "I" that feeds off my authentic anxieties and money worries while also exaggerating these negative feelings to the extreme. Putting my most personal experiences down on paper transforms them in a way that I hope will make it easier for others to connect with them. What's more, by writing my worries and anxieties down, I create a distance from them that robs them of their power. As long as I continue writing, I'll keep my fear at bay.

Thank you:
Beate Söntgen, Jakob Lehrecke, Margaux Graw,
Merlin Carpenter, Jörg-Uwe Albig, Violaine Huisman

Isabelle Graw

Fear and Money

Published by Sternberg Press

Translated from the German by Ben Caton

Editor: Anita Iannacchione

Proofreading: Danielle N. Carter

Design: Studio Markus Weisbeck

Printing: Tallinn Book Printers, Estonia

Cover image: Edvard Munch, *Angst*, 1896. Image number: MM.G.00568-03.
Photo: Munchmuseet / Halvor Bjørngård.

ISBN 978-1-915609-69-4

© 2025 Isabelle Graw, Sternberg Press

All rights reserved, including the right of reproduction in whole or in part in any form.

Originally published as *Angst und Geld* (Spector Books, 2024)

Distributed by The MIT Press, Art Data, Les presses du réel, and Idea Books

Sternberg Press

71–75 Shelton Street

UK–London WC2H 9JQ

www.sternberg-press.com